POWER PLAY

POWER PLAY

A collection of twenty erotic stories

Edited by Miranda Forbes

Published by Xcite Books Ltd – 2011
ISBN 9781907761720

Printed and bound in the UK

Cover design by
Madamadari

Contents

Power Lunch
by Rachel Kramer Bussel

One of the perks of running your own business is having an assistant, a person whose job is to cater to your every whim. I've never been good at taking orders, in or out of the bedroom, so running my own business was a natural fit. So was naming it after myself; I, Claudia, LLC. Yes, I have a bit of an ego, but I like the fact that my name is adorned on all our products, my signature scrawl sported across the tubes of hundreds of thousands of lipsticks and mascaras, imprinted across shiny compacts, along with skincare products, shampoo, conditioner, you name it.

But the best thing about our continuing growth is having someone who's on demand whenever I need him. In the early days, I had a part-time secretary, whose job also covered attending to the needs of the other executives and greeting people at our front door; I couldn't afford someone full-time to cater to my whims, but once we started getting picked up by the likes of Sephora and major department stores, being known to hundreds of thousands of consumers and regularly featured in magazines, I was able to hire Patrick, who's been with me now for four years.

Now, Patrick is my assistant, not my boyfriend, so I get all the perks of having the latter, one with a hot ass, eager tongue and huge cock, without any of the drama. I'm 32; he's 24, with a baby face but a wise-beyond-his-years demeanour. He doesn't get jealous when I go out with other people, doesn't feel emasculated by my success, doesn't ask pesky, annoying questions. I still date, and was even living with a guy until a few months ago, but that's just not the same. Patrick likes me, and likes working for me, as well as working under me, whether that means me sitting on his face or grinding against him to give myself an orgasm or two.

Actually, he more than likes it; 'Use me, please,' he'll say when I shove him up against my desk or into a chair or up against the wall. I haven't had tons of time to date as I've climbed my own corporate ladder, but I have learnt a thing or two about submissive men, and can spot them in a crowded subway car or across a room at a cocktail party. They carry themselves in a way that's just a touch different than your average I've-got-a-big-cock-and-want-to-show-it-to-you straight guy. I prefer the type of guy who wants to be told how small his cock is, no matter the reality, the kind who wants to be shrunken down to size rather than puffed up into an inflated version of himself. Thankfully, Patrick does, indeed, have a big cock – one of the biggest I've ever seen – but his manhood doesn't depend on proving its length, but rather on me using it to my full satisfaction.

With Patrick, I can have long lunches, on-the-spot massages (foot and back, as well as more intimate ones) and generally get off on the high of telling him what to do. Now, I wouldn't subject a man who wasn't into that sort of thing to the kinds of things I ask of Patrick, because that just wouldn't be fair. Instead, I found myself the cutest sub I could out of the applicant pool, and I pay him handsomely for his services. He's earned raises and bonuses over the years, generally when his performance has gone above and beyond, like when, of his own accord, he stays with his head buried between my legs even after I've come, just because he wants to, because he loves my taste and wants to give me that extra climax that'll make my day that just much better, or when he goes and buys me lingerie or cupcakes.

Sometimes I add little bonus tasks, just because I can; maybe he'll have to wear my lipstick while running his errands, going to the same shops and restaurants he regularly makes pickups for me, letting them wonder who exactly this hot man is with the deepest crimson on his lips.

I like to keep him on his toes, and enjoy every opportunity I can to make sure everyone who sees me knows not just how successful I am, but that I've parlayed that success into possessing a cutie-pie like Patrick. Possession isn't just nine-tenths of the law; it's the ultimate corporate status symbol. Just like you see men with white hair flaunting their extremely perky secretaries with their extremely perky, often enlarged breasts, as a way of saying "fuck you" to any other men venturing into his office, I use Patrick as a way to confirm my success. Just seeing him sitting behind his desk, his brown hair tucked behind his ears, smooth-shaven cheeks looking ready to pinch, is enough to get me out of bed even when I'd rather call in sick. There's no one telling me I can't, but somehow Patrick manages to make me feel better

Today I decided that I wanted a special lunch, from my favourite high-end place, the ultimate Manhattan see-and-be-seen restaurant. You usually can't get a reservation on the same day, but I've instructed Patrick to do whatever he can to make the various hostesses of my favourite places happy, and he has done whatever it took to make sure that if I want a table, I get it. Maybe some bosses prize discretion, but I've enjoyed hearing about the after-hours blowjobs, spankings and beatings he's given and taken to prove his devotion to the job. I also think these adventures have taught him well that to get ahead in the world, you have to be open, agreeable, ready for anything, and it can't hurt to have a wide sexual appetite.

Usually I get my lunches delivered so I can close my door and work in peace, masterminding next season's colours, overseeing our ads, posting on my blog about the latest make-up news, checking numbers and simply enjoying some downtime. I'm not a huge social eater, so when I told Patrick we were taking a long lunch, he knew something was up. Most of my staff are allowed to get away with casual clothing, but not Patrick. I like to see him in a dress shirt and slacks every day, his shoes shiny and perfect. He can afford to buy the designer brands I prefer, and he knows if he comes in wearing yesterday's rumpled clothes or some old sweater and jeans, he'll be sent home.

I get off on the power of knowing he'll do what I say, no matter how bizarre, as evidenced by the time I told him to come in wearing a hot pink tie I'd had delivered to his apartment, along with matching pants. He did it, and no one dared say a word in front of me.

This time, though, I had a definite plan in mind. I wanted to push Patrick as far as I can, and the mere thought was making my pussy cream. To prep him, I took out my breast, positioning it strategically against my navy silk blazer, and took a photo, then emailed it to him. I run the company, so there's nobody telling me what I can and can't email. The subject line to him read, "Ready for lunch?" I know he loves to nurse on my tits, and I enjoy it just as much.

He knocked discreetly on my door, and when I let him in, I saw his massive dick pressing against the softness of his pants, and suddenly I was hungry for more than wild bear tortellini, but I couldn't let my appetite for cock get in the way of today's mission. 'Get my coat,' I barked dismissively, because that is how I speak to him, and he did, holding it so I can easily slide my arms, arms I spend hours toning with a trainer each week, into the sleeves.

My five-inch black heels clicked on the ground as Patrick walked a discreet distance behind me. Our offices aren't too far from this very famous bistro, and though we could've taken a cab, I liked the looks that we drew as we walked, with Patrick remaining a few deferential steps behind me. I snapped my fingers when we hit the sidewalk and he handed me a cigarette, then flipped the lighter open and lit it for me. I will fully admit that I only wanted a few puffs; I wouldn't even call myself a recreational smoker, but more a kinky one. I love how fast Patrick can get my smoke lit, love the ritual of taking that first powerful inhale, then turning just enough to blow it back in his face. Nothing says power trip like wearing my brightest red lipstick and holding a long, extra-skinny cigarette in my hand – well, except for when we're at a posh event and I make Patrick hold my smokes for me as I'm smoking them, having to stand nearby to hold the cigarette to my lips every time I want another puff.

We arrived at the ornate door to the restaurant, where Patrick opened the door for me and ushered us inside. We spied many famous faces, such as Barbara Walters and Kathie Lee Gifford, as we were led to our seats, in a fashionable area, near those who radiated wealth and power. A few tables over, I spied a prominent politician with a much younger woman who was decidedly not his wife.

'He'll sit here, near me,' I instructed our waiter, Vincent, as I pointed to the seat adjacent to me, rather than across the table. They were generous about giving us a table for four for our party of two; that's what happens when you seek out the sexual sweet spots of the most powerful maitre d's in the restaurant business. Patrick slid into the seat, then looked up at me expectantly. 'Relax,' I said, then patted his knee, keeping my right hand there as I opened my menu. 'Champagne sounds good, don't you think?' It was a rhetorical question, because if it sounded good to me, it would sound good to Patrick; that's how we worked.

'So, tell me something good,' I said, as I perused the menu for both of us. Oysters and the tortellini for an appetizer, pan-roasted black cod for Patrick, and a burger for me. I didn't need to study the options long to make those selections. I could've chosen something more refined, but few foods put me in the mood more than a medium rare, juicy burger, as if recharging my animalistic instincts. I felt

Patrick twitch beneath my hand as I placed the order; he knows exactly how red meat makes me feel.

'Well, I just redid my closets,' he said, then shut up immediately when he saw the look on my face, one that clearly said, *I don't care about your fucking closets*. No, what I wanted was his cock, or rather, stories about it. That was one of the other perks of the job, that I got to hear about who he screwed outside of our arrangement; I wasn't egotistical enough to tie him up in that way (though other means were perfectly acceptable), and besides, then I would've been deprived of the gossip that can only be created after an act of dirty, filthy sex.

'Oh. Well, I got a blowjob. In a bathroom. From a guy.' He said it all really fast, then looked up at me for a second, like I was going to scold him, but really, that was in his head, because far from wanting to berate him, I wanted to hear more. This was the first time I'd heard anything about Patrick being intimate with another guy.

'Details please,' I said, just as Vincent slid two flutes of champagne in front of us. Usually I'm the dirty martini type, but I wanted to keep the mood celebratory, and didn't want to get quite as drunk as a martini would've made me. I shifted so I could slip off one of my very sharp heels and press my foot against Patrick's calf.

'I was at this party, some PR thing you got invited to and didn't want to attend. I went stag and figured I'd see someone I knew. It was mostly women, but there were some guys, and just as I was trying to decide which type of cheese from the abundant array to spear my toothpick into, this older guy leant close to me and said, 'You like stinky cheese, do you?' when I hovered over a particularly ripe blue cheese.' He paused here to take a sip of his champagne, and I tilted my head back to finish my glass. I used to drink my ass off in college and the few years after that in a buzzed blur, intent on getting wasted as quickly as possible, the altered state brought on by alcohol being both the means and the end. Now, as a slightly older woman, and certainly a richer one, I knew better, knew that savouring the slow slide into that heightened awareness was what it was all about. Couple that with a doting servant whose cock was at my command and I might as well have been high.

'Keep going,' I said, brushing my toes against his cock for a moment, just to check and make sure he was as hard as I suspected he was.

'I just smiled, not sure what to say, and took the cheese and put it in my mouth. He walked around the table and stood right behind me and whispered in my ear, 'I bet you like to swallow.' It was weird, because guys have hit on me before, but I just never felt anything, not even a hint of excitement, but this guy did something to me. I didn't even look around to see if anyone was watching us; I just leant back against him, letting my ass rest against his cock.'

I interrupted him. 'Undo your zipper; let your cock hang out.'

He gave me a "you-can't-be-serious" look. 'I'm perfectly fucking serious; this is my lunch and I'm going to do it my way. Unless you want me to find an assistant who's actually willing to assist me.'

He stared straight at me, his gaze stony, clearly not quite as into the idea of taking his cock out in public as I was; that is one of the wonderful things about being so completely in control. I not only get to dictate what happens, but to teach the younger generation a thing or two. Because I knew, without a doubt, that once his cock was out in the open air, Patrick would like it– or at least, his cock would. 'Continue,' I said, waving a hand in the air just as our appetizers arrived.

My wandering foot, which I'd placed in the vicinity of his crotch, made sure that he was doing what I'd instructed. As he said, 'And then he full-on kissed my neck, and I liked it. He was definitely the one putting the moves on me, and for a second I thought about you commanding me to submit to him.' His voice trembled as he pulled down his zipper and my toes met his cock. It was as if the thrill went straight to my pussy, and I had to work to keep my face composed lest I give away our secret, though I had a feeling our waiter wouldn't mind knowing about our bit of naughtiness. I teased Patrick's cock, glad I'd been rigorous with my workouts so I could control my leg as I balanced it straight ahead while I casually lifted my glass, tilted my head, and prepared to listen as Patrick revealed his story of submitting to a man.

'I thought about you watching as he kissed the back of my neck, and when he turned me around to kiss me full on the lips, I just went with it.' I heard a throat-clearing, and saw that Vincent had appeared with a bread basket. I smiled at him seductively, hoping he'd heard that last bit.

I could smell the scent of freshly baked bread wafting from beneath the folds of a pristine napkin. 'Could you uncover that for us?' I said, flirting with the rapid blinking of my eyelashes, the purr in my voice and the smile just barely curving my lips. 'You never know what could be hiding under a white cloth.' Vincent looked up at me, coughed discreetly, then made the act of displaying the rolls into what I can only describe as foreplay. I studied his hands blatantly, not for his sake, but for Patrick's.

'Anything else, ma'am?'

'Some butter, please,' I said, 'and make sure it's melted until it's hot and gooey. Thank you.'

I flexed my foot against Patrick's cock as he reached for a roll. I slapped his hand away. 'You'll wait until I have my butter, won't you?'

'Yes, Claudia, of course.'

'Good, now keep going. I want to hear what you let Mr Sexpot do to you.'

'We started kissing right there, even though my face was hot. These were people I knew mostly from work, and I wondered what they would think. When we paused, he

8

noticed how red I was. "A blusher ... I like that. Do you want to go somewhere more private?" I just nodded, and soon we were in the bathroom, which was better, except that it was the only one in the place, so I knew people would soon be wanting to get in. I was a little panicked because he'd been so aggressive.' The more he talked, the more I wiggled my foot, even inching my seat closer so I could press the entire sole of my foot, not just the ball, against his package. Vincent arrived with the butter.

'You can set it right here, darlin',' I instructed, patting the spot next to me, where he might see my raised leg. He brushed against my side as he set down the small bowl, filled with a puddle of melted butter.

'Well, it turned out he didn't want to fuck me, but to suck my cock.'

'Was it as hard as it is now?' I asked.

'Yes, it was. He told me to take it out and show it to him, and I did, just like that.' Patrick's pale face was flushed a deep red, and I smiled as I shifted slightly to include his balls in my fun. 'We both stroked my dick for a while,' he said, while I tore a roll in half and dipped it into the butter, before taking a bite, re-dipping, and offering the bread to Patrick. He opened his mouth and took a dainty bite, staring back at me the whole while.

I pulled my foot down, slipping it back into my shoe, and noticed his hand go to his lap. 'Leave it,' I snapped. Vincent, who seemed to be vying for most attentive waiter status, was back with our appetizers. 'You can set them both on my side,' I told him.

When he'd departed, I took an oyster, tipped my head back and let it slide down my throat. 'Delicious. Why don't you have one?' Then I plucked another and leant forward to serve it to Patrick, making sure a bit of the juice dribbled from the shell straight into his lap.

'I–' he started, but I was sliding my nail along the oyster's edge to separate it from the shell, and then it was

9

rushing down his throat. I thought about the way my pussy juices did the same when I sat on his face, the way he delighted in me mashing myself against his open lips.

I wanted to kiss him just then; it was a tender moment, or as tender a moment as one can have in the middle of a restaurant. I leant forward and whispered in his ear. 'You can put it away now.' I knew he'd have to do so beneath the table, and the fumbling caused him to blush even more, especially when, though we hadn't touched the tortellini, Vincent was already back with our cod and burger. 'Patrick will have the cod,' I instructed, and he reached for the plate, as if by being helpful to our waiter he'd become the model diner, not the exhibitionist one.

I caught the look Vincent shot him, one of lust and appraisal, before Vincent reached for my burger. 'Condiments, ma'am?'

'Call me Claudia, and I'll take some relish,' I said.

'Please feel free to start,' I told Patrick, realising we'd be there for ever if I fed him his food between bites of my burger, and got the rest of the story. 'And speak up.' I gave him a beatific smile as I helped myself to some tortellini, glad I'd worn my long-lasting red lipstick.

Patrick took a bite of the cod then went on. 'I was so hard I thought I might come at any moment, but when the guy actually got on his knees and started sucking me off, I didn't explode as I'd have thought I would. I watched him, and tried to forget about the crowd outside, and just enjoy his mouth. He wasn't trying to swallow the whole thing at once, but moving slowly and, I saw, touching himself at the same time.' Vincent appeared with my relish, and handed it to me silently, as if he didn't want to interrupt the heated nature of the story. I smiled at him and gestured to Patrick to continue. 'It was so good. The best blowjob I've ever had,' he said, then glanced at me, stricken, 'I mean, except for yours.' It's not something I do often, but as a special reward, I've sucked Patrick's cock a few times over the years, usually on his birthday.

'It was just amazing, and knowing that he was so into it made me bold. I grabbed the back of his head and, supporting myself on the sink, thrust my hips upward into him.' I spread relish on my burger, then took a big bite and chewed while I listened to the culmination of his story, about how he thought he could swallow all of the man's come, but wound up having it spill down his chin and onto his shirt. I was sure that Patrick's cock was still hard, both because I knew how talking dirty aroused him, and because anyone's cock would be hard from listening to such a hot story. In fact, when I looked up, I noticed two women next to us staring toward me enviously; they quickly looked away when my gaze swept over them. I wound up eating more quickly than I'd planned, because the tale, and the burger, were so rich and juicy, and before I knew it I was done, and ready to leave. Patrick had barely touched his food, but I flagged down Vincent and handed him my Amex Black card.

'Will you be needing a doggy bag?'

'That would be fitting, I suppose, for Patrick here. He can be a slow eater at times. But I'm in a bit of a hurry and don't want to delay us any further. I have urgent business to attend to. Thanks, sugar.' I winked at Vincent and let Patrick get in a few more mouthfuls, then signed the check and swept out of the restaurant. I decided to extend our lunch to one of my favourite hotels, which was conveniently only a few blocks away. They know me there and their customer service is outstanding, so we had a room within minutes of walking through the door. Patrick didn't question me; I knew my schedule was clear for the rest of the afternoon.

'Since you got such a fabulous blowjob last night, I want you to give me one right now,' I said, stripping off my clothes until I was clad only in my garter and stockings. I'd have used my panties to tie Patrick's hands behind his back, but they were the kind that are barely more than a scrap of fabric. 'Keep your hands behind your back. And you better do a good job to thank me for lunch.' Patrick worked his tongue along my slit, going slowly, getting me used to his attentions. He knows I like for him to start slow, so I can fully relax into what he's doing. For me to properly enjoy cunnilingus, I have to get out of domme mode just a little and into woman mode; of course, he knows I'm still in charge, but I can surrender just a bit to his tongue, just as he surrenders to the pleasure that eating me out gives him.

That is the real secret to our harmony as lovers and boss/employee: we both enjoy the dance as much as its culmination, we both know what drives us, in the world, in the office, and with each other. As he sucked on my clit, while I brought my hands to the back of his head, tugging on his hair, like I imagine he'd done with his anonymous lover from the previous night, I smiled. Being able to take a break from the workday and get my pussy eaten was the ultimate power trip. 'Fingers,' I said, snapping mine, and Patrick brought his right hand from behind his back and slid two fingers into my pussy, curling them just so. I held onto him tightly as I trembled, unlocking the most special power of all as my orgasm quaked through me. I screamed, and felt the noise ripple through the room, through the walls, and out into the universe. 'Bon appétit,' I whispered, and pulled Patrick up for a kiss, before calling in and letting the others at the office know they could all go home for the day. You see, power doesn't always corrupt; sometimes it erupts, which I planned to keep doing for the rest of the day, with a little help from my trusty assistant.

Amy
by Alex Severn

She knew today was the day. She had thought about it enough by now.

It was going to be a hot afternoon and they would all be in the garden. His garden while his parents were away. And after all, Helen and Jim *had* asked her to keep an eye on Joe. She smiled at the way Helen had said, 'I know he's 19 but ... well, you know what boys are like ... just make sure he doesn't wreck the place. We've told him he can have his mates round a couple of times but we don't want any wild parties. I mean, the noise wouldn't be welcomed by any of the neighbours, you included, would it? Look after him for us OK?'

Maybe it was the phrase "look after him" that finally decided her although, in her more honest moments, she had to admit she had been thinking about enjoying a young man for a long time. Well, young *men* to be more accurate.

As she dressed Amy gave a thorough appraisal of her body.

Slim – good figure, maybe her boobs were a little big for her own liking but most men wanted that, didn't they? Her hair was auburn; she made sure it was in good condition. She eased herself out of her jeans and, before she slipped her summer skirt on, she smiled at her long tanned legs. Her knickers were tiny but only a minute's hesitation convinced her to take them off, revealing a neatly shaven brown bush.

Her smile deepened as she thought of their reaction when they first saw her pussy ... Her labia would be wet by then and as she unclasped her bra and let it fall to the floor she knew that, although her nipples were starting to stiffen now, when the boys had their first sight of them they would be diamond hard which would only make those young cocks all the harder for her.

She paused enjoying the sight of her own naked body and, almost without thinking, her right hand strayed towards her clit but she mentally chided herself. Today she mustn't work herself off. The boys would take care of that for her, although she knew she may have to teach them how ...

She decided on a light blue summer dress with no bra but a tiny thong. She was glad she had freshly shaved her pussy. The dress was short enough to cover the tops of her thighs but little else. Her cleavage was on show but she had other dresses which showed it more. No perfume – it was hot and she knew the smell of her as a woman was more potent for a young man than anything a manufacturer could come up with.

So by 8 p.m. she was ready.

She took up her position in her upstairs window and it wasn't long before his "guests" arrived. It had been all too simple to find out which day he had invited the boys round the day after his parents flew off on their holiday. She had done her other research well too; although Joe didn't have a girlfriend some of the lads did, but this was a night for men only apparently.

God were they in for a surprise!

Time ticked by as she watched them discreetly. First kicking a ball around and swearing loudly, then a vague attempt at a barbecue which never properly got started. She amused herself by mentally undressing them.

The tall blond lad was a likely candidate for the local girls she felt, athletic and with an air of confidence. A boy who looked younger than the rest interested her, his close cropped brown hair and his surprisingly muscular chest which was revealed when he got too hot ... but Joe was her first choice; he had a cheeky sweet way about him. She suddenly wished she had invested in binoculars so she could see if he had an erection building, but then she laughed at herself – they were just fooling around together; if they had known a mature woman was eyeing them up like this it would have been different. They would know soon enough ...

When she saw them go back inside as the light was fading she knew it was time to act. Amy made her preparations efficiently and carefully.

She went across to the house, up the gravel path and knocked, mentally rehearsing the right words, the right tone.

The door opened and Joe stood there.

'Oh sorry to bother you, love, but ... I need a couple of strong young men. I couldn't drag you over to help me, could I? I hate to disturb your party, but if you and one of your friends could ...'

God it was so easy. Within seconds Joe had recruited the cute little blond boy (how lucky was she?!) and she was letting them in her front door.

'It's my room. I know I'm stupid but I was trying to move stuff around and I've knocked over the wardrobe and now I can't move it back. Wonder you didn't hear the bang – I thought it might drop through the floor!'

'No problem, Mrs Davies, we can lift it, can't we, Gareth?'

'Oh thank you, Joe, come up then.'

She needed to go first, of course, making sure they had a good view of her legs and a few glimpses of her knickers as the little dress rode up as she slowly went up the stairs. She had to step over the prone wardrobe; she had made sure it was really awkward to manoeuvre past it. As she had to alter her body position to do so, she could hardly keep the smug grin off her face at their reaction to the sight of her stooping

15

body revealing most of her breasts and the way her tiny thong was even more exposed made them dart glances at each other.

Amy was now standing by her bed while the two boys were at either side of the wardrobe.

'If you can lift it up maybe and just stand it back by the wall ... but wait, it's heavy, let me take stuff out of it first, OK?'

Amy took her time, of course. She wanted them to see the underwear, the black basque, the suspender belts, the tiny things she had placed prominently among all her usual clothes. She lingered over the handcuffs and the silver chain longest of all. Everything went on the bed. Joe and his mate were goggle-eyed and she revelled in their expressions. She only had to pretend she wasn't aware of the effect her toys and she herself was having on them both.

It didn't take them long to play removal men – in face, they were finished quicker than she had hoped so she knew she had to act quickly now.

Amy had carefully made sure a belt and a dress had been discarded by her bed, near her feet and, as she had practised enough times, she caught her foot in them both and catapulted forward, launching into Joe's arms.

He instinctively caught hold of her as she gave a slightly over-theatrical squeal. Amy slowly steadied herself against his body, easing then tilting her hips to his groin.

Time to move now.

She grinned broadly and, she hoped, seductively.

'Well, well ... does moving furniture get you that excited, young man?'

Joe blushed scarlet, no idea what to say or how to react, but it was all in her script.

Amy gently placed one, two fingers on the crotch of his jeans and stroked the length of his fast-stiffening erection. Then placing her other hand on his bum, she almost savagely unzipped him and, as he gasped, she roughly rammed her fingers inside his boxers, manipulating, manoeuvring his cock, playing with his head and foreskin.

'Oh fuck ...' was all Joe could manage.

'In time, sweetheart, in time,' was the woman's reply.

Turning her head so she could gauge the blond boy's reaction (open mouthed, sweating and panting), Amy summarily pulled down Joe's jeans, then his boxers so he was left there, both garments around his ankles, his thick long cock now jutting out as if to meet her.

'Well, you may as well take them off. In fact get that shirt off too ... Let me see what you have to offer, Joe.'

The young man couldn't obey quickly enough. And there he stood, naked, sweat pooling on his chest, cock sprouting from his thick forest of dark hair.

Next step.

'OK, honey, we can't have you standing there missing out on all the fun, can we? Strip now, everything off.'

Gareth hesitated slightly, whether from reluctance to show her his body or embarrassment at being naked in front of his mate, but Amy didn't care what it was – she was in charge and they had to learn that.

'Do you want me tonight? Do you want to see me stripped and fuck me? If you don't do as you're told, you are going back next door to spend a long night regretting what you missed, OK?'

The perfect threat.

Gareth could hardly tear his clothes off quickly enough and she laughed softly as he stood there before her so she could examine his body.

He had a better physique than Joe, looked stronger, more muscular. He had a light sheen of fair hair on his chest and his pubes were a light gold colour. His cock was definitely thicker and wider than Joe's, and he had a huge pair of hairy balls that she could tell, even from a couple of yards away, were tightening with lust for her.

She smiled sweetly at one, then the other.

'Would you like to see me now, boys? You've had a pretty good view so far but there is *so* much more to enjoy, trust me.'

Neither of them could speak. They were holding their breath and, Gareth in particular, stood like a waxwork figure as if he felt moving would break the spell.

Amy eased her little dress over her head and let it drop to the floor. She knew most men were mesmerised by her tits and she bathed in the sheer pubescent lust that radiated from them both as their eyes devoured them. Her coral brown nipples stood to attention and she arched her back enough so they seemed to be pointing directly at Joe.

Her tiny thong was still in place and they may just as well have been begging, pleading with her to take it off and give them the view they most wanted.

She knew they were totally and completely at her mercy now and she was going to wallow in it.

'If you want to see my pussy – my wet, open, soft pussy – you have to earn it, boys. Joe, go over to your friend and kiss him on the lips, go on now ...'

Joe stood transfixed but summoned up his courage and his voice.

'No way, we're not gay.'

Amy smiled but there was a light of warning in her eyes.

'Nobody's saying you are, dear boy. But you see, ever since I watched this gay porn film, it's been, well, a little fantasy of mine to witness two strong, sexy guys get it on together. I want to see you close up, your bodies pressing together. It won't do you any harm, will it? I won't tell any of your mates and you two aren't going to shout about it, right?'

Neither boy moved so she knew she had to be more domineering, make them choose quickly now.

'Listen now, both of you. OK, Joe, Gareth. I'm not asking you to become lovers or move in together. I want you to entertain me and, if you do, believe me, you'll get your reward.'

On her last syllable, Amy moved her right hand to the top of her thong and started to gently lift it allowing her fingers to stray inside and towards her pussy.

Suddenly, Gareth sprang into action.

He put shaking hands on Joe's shoulders and planted a rough, hard kiss on his mate's lips. Almost recoiling, Joe began to wipe his mouth with the back of his hand.

'Come off it, you two, I want to see a bit of passion here. Joe, kiss him properly and make it last a bit. Do it for me.'

She came up close to them both then – they could have reached out and played with those dark brown nubs but they both knew she wouldn't allow it unless they co-operated with her wishes.

Decisively, Joe grabbed Gareth by the shoulders and moved his face then his lips to touch the other's.

They were locked into a kiss and they both felt her hand on their bums, pressing them together.

Amy knew they wanted to break clear of each other, hoping they had done her bidding but she wasn't going to allow that now.

Sweating with desire herself now, she half parted them but only to allow space for each of her hands to grasp and fondle their cocks. She felt their arousal, heard them gulp and moan and she felt how wet she already was. Amy knew they were transfixed and more was to come for them.

'OK, boys. You can stop snogging for me now. My, my, didn't that make you good and hard?'

She saw their furious rebellious glares but was safe in the certainty their rebellion would stay silent.

'Let me see you both wank for me now. Do it – I want to see you come for me. Pump those big thick cocks for Amy.'

Apparently this was an easier request for them, but she smiled at how they kept trying not to look at each other's bodies as they yanked, stroked and pulled at their rock-hard shafts.

Joe came first. He spurted out all over her bedroom carpet, thick sticky fluid oozing from his cock. Amy waited until Gareth had caught him up and then treated them to her filthiest smile again.

'Well done. Nice to see you come for an old lady like me. Would you like to see me come for you now?'

A rhetorical question but anyway they seemed almost incapable of speech by now.

So she slid her hand right down inside her thong and began to play with her lips, her clit, widening her legs, easing her body backwards and forwards, drinking in their hungry desperate eyes, drawing them in, watching their helpless enslavement for her as if the world had suddenly vanished.

Amy hadn't been absolutely sure how she would play the next act but she had to admit they had been very dutiful – she really could do whatever she wanted them to. But she decided to treat them now ...

Throwing her body back onto her bed, she lifted her long legs skywards and peeled off her thong, opening her legs wide to display her glistening pussy.

'Oh shit, you're fucking fantastic.' Gareth's words but both their minds spoke.

Amy increased the pace of her probing fingers; she had inserted three of them by now, her cunt was a cavern, an Aladdin's cave of treasures for them to wonder at. She teased the hard nub of her clit. She explored, opened and proudly displayed her pink-purple labia for her audience. As she felt herself coming she screamed her triumphal orgasm to herself, not to them. Amy scooped out fingers full of cunt juice and held them out to their eager mouths. Gareth devoured it as if he had been starved for weeks.

Breathing heavily, she smiled again, softer, more accommodating this time.

'Well then ... what a dilemma we have. Two fit young men, hard and horny, and just one woman to be fucked.

Whatever shall we do? Toss a coin for who fucks me? Or toss yourselves off again maybe?'

She grinned at their expressions. They really believed she was going to choose one and send the other home – and no amount of friendship would heal that rift, would it?

'Don't look so worried. This is a game for three to play. After all, I do have two holes that need a good filling, don't I? Well actually I have three but, er, that's for another day maybe ...'

It was hard to keep a straight face as she watched them absorb what she was offering so she rolled over onto her stomach and tilted her arse up toward their faces.

'To save you the agony of choice, I will decide.'

Amy passed long enough to let them swallow hard and try not to look at each other and then said, 'Joe, you can fuck my cunt and Gareth can have my sweet arse. I know you are such good friends, nice that you can share a good fuck, isn't it? You'll never enjoy a better one, trust me, boys.'

Amy had to admit after they had staggered back to Joe's house that she hadn't expected them to be able to satisfy her so well.

Joe had thrusted away manfully, she had clamped his cock in her generous soft folds, rocking him back and forth, easing him in deeper. But Gareth! That young man was going to make a lot of women very happy over the next few years, that was for sure! Of course she had had a few cocks up her arse before but he really did grind deep inside; she'd kept backing onto him, no easy feat with Joe's cock driving into her cunt too. At one point Amy felt their cocks were almost touching through the soft membrane between her cunt and her arse ... and, God, she loved every second! OK, she had had to order Joe to twist her nipples and scream at him to be rougher but she could live with that, couldn't she? And the way Gareth's big hairy balls slapped against her arse drove her crazy.

Funny how the silence fell over them all as her orgasm swept over her body – as if they all knew the play was over. Back to reality.

In all fairness, Helen and Jim *had* asked her to look after their son ... and that's exactly what she'd done, right?

Well, what were neighbours for?

Highland Games
by Bimbo Ross

By the time they arrived at their first campsite, in the northern reaches of Scotland, the sun was already sitting on the western horizon, casting pale orange rays across the sea. As Ian pulled on the handbrake he reached across towards Carrie and ran his fingers along her naked thigh. They crept under her shorts and he felt the silkiness of her panties underneath; there was a warm dampness to them. Carrie gave his hand a playful slap.

'Patience, darling.'

He groaned his disappointment but removed his hand. Carrie lifted her long limbs out of the compact BMW, raised her arms in the air and stretched like a lynx. Ian, already out and standing by the driver's door, watched her, the glint in his eyes unmistakable.

'Later, you naughty boy,' she stalled once more, and turned her back on him, taking in the scene around them. 'Oh, this is perfect, Ian.' Carrie looked up at the heather-strewn hillside immediately behind the camping area they were standing in, and back to the beach again. She sighed deeply. 'You've done good, boy.'

Ian grinned. 'Well, you can reward me later, honey bun, but first I guess we have to get this tent up before it gets dark.'

They had been allocated a spot on the outer edges of a scraggy field that had been turned into a camping site several years ago by a shrewd farmer. After purchasing the land, he decided that there couldn't be much difference between managing campers and managing sheep, and quickly discovered that the former, although actually more demanding, was also much more lucrative.

About 50 tents and caravans were scattered around the rough pastureland and, being the last to arrive for the evening, Ian and Carrie found themselves allocated a spot farthest away from the amenities. The slight inconvenience of the extra walk to the toilet and shower block was more than compensated for by the privacy of their pitch. Sometimes they made a noise.

Since it was the first night of their holiday, it was also the first time they'd put the tent up. In fact, it was the first time either of them had ever put any tent up. It wasn't as easy as it said on the box.

A wind got up while they were in the middle of erecting it and Carrie suddenly felt the corner she was holding on to, being ripped from her hand. She let out a small shriek as her half of the tent went soaring into the sky. Ian had to quickly strengthen his hold in order to keep the whole thing from disappearing across the sands and into the sea.

'Aw, fuck! Can't you keep hold of that?'

'Sorry, the wind just took it away. And don't swear at me.'

'I'm not swearing at you, darling,' Ian replied in a patronising tone. 'I'm swearing at the frigging wind.' He hammered in the tent peg to secure his corner and came round to Carrie's side to help her regain control. He retrieved the flapping material and placed it securely in her hand, taking her other hand and closing them both tightly over the fabric. 'Now, don't let it go this time.'

'I didn't *let* it go the last time,' Carrie protested. 'It was the wind.'

Ian ignored her and returned to his task. He managed to

get a second peg in, and was coming round to Carrie's side to do hers when a gust of wind repeated its previous felony.

'Fucking hell, can't you just hold on to it?' he screamed at her.

'No, I can't. Just fucking do it yourself then!' Carrie stamped her foot as she swore at Ian and stormed off to the rear of the car.

At that moment, an elderly couple materialised at Ian's side. The silver-haired man addressed Ian while the woman sent conciliatory smiles in Carrie's direction.

'Hello there, I think we're your neighbours. I'm Albert and this is my wife, Gladys,' he said.

Ian looked at him askance, astonished when Albert held out his hand to make the introduction. Couldn't he see that he had his hands full?

Although Albert laughed when he realised the foolishness of his gesture, and put his hand back by his side, he still carried on chatting. 'We've just come back from the town, you know. It's a lovely night for a stroll along the beach. We just kept walking and walking until we ended up at this lovely little village. Didn't we, dear?' He looked at Gladys for confirmation and she repaid him with a gracious nod. 'You should have a look some time,' he suggested. Ian still hadn't said a word as he stood there frantically trying to keep hold of the offending corner of the tent. The old guy finally seemed to take notice of Ian's predicament. 'You haven't done this before, have you, lad?' He walked around the canvas heap that Ian was now standing on. 'Do you need a hand?'

By the time the two men had erected the tent, Carrie had calmed down enough to thank their "neighbours", at the same time declining their offer of tea, on the grounds that they wanted an early night, grinning at each other in anticipation as they made their excuses.

'Well, if there's anything you need, just call out,' Gladys offered as she and her husband disappeared through the flaps of their tent.

Ian held his hand up to the barman, pointed to their two drinks and gestured for two more of the same.

'No, no more for me,' Carrie quickly said, 'not if we have to walk back along the beach.'

After getting their tent sorted, they'd decided to drive down to the village and get something to eat rather than risk the gas stove. Having failed their first task of the day, they were reluctant to chance another cock-up. What they hadn't considered though, was how drunk they might get – too drunk to drive back. And although she wasn't looking forward to the return walk, Carrie was quite keen to get to their tent, and the pleasures that lay therein. She chivvied Ian along again. 'Don't you think you've had enough too? You don't want to become incapable, do you?'

Ian felt a warm sensation rush through his body as Carrie snuggled in closer to him. He'd intended to plant a kiss on her mouth but it missed and landed on her cheek. Maybe it was time for them to make a move.

'Let's have one more for the road.'

They were glad the wind was behind them, shuttling them along the beach as they headed back to the campsite. They could just make out its lights now, about 50 metres away.

'Brrr, it's getting cold,' Carrie complained as she leaned in closer to Ian. He stopped and took her into his arms, slipping his hand inside her pullover.

'Oh, but you're nice and hot in here.' He could feel her nipple hardening against his touch. He moved the palm of his hand across to her other breast, felt it equally receptive, then brought his mouth down to hers; her tongue was warm. He tried to prise his fingers down the inside of her jeans, but they were too tight. Ian's were looser and Carrie managed to get her hand inside his and take a tentative grip of his growing dick, but her hand was cold on his hot prick and he shivered a little despite the sizzling pleasure that ran through him. 'If it weren't so cold, I'd suggest a skinny dip,' he laughed. 'But I'm fucking freezing out here. Let's get back to the tent.'

'OK, I'll race you.' Carrie's hand was out of his jeans and she was five yards ahead of him before Ian reacted and began to chase after her. They had to scramble through some scraggy, unlit sand dunes, avoiding high tufts of rye grass, before they reached the edge of the campsite and entered the park through a creaky wooden gate built into the fence. Carrie let the gate swing behind her as she rushed ahead. It almost bowled Ian over.

'OK, if that's how you want to play, young lady,' he shouted, 'then first one there has to open the Glenfiddich.'

'I'm glad you remembered the extra pillows,' Ian said, as he arranged three of them, one on top of the other in the centre of the airbed. They'd blown it up fully so that it was quite firm underneath them. 'Let's start with your panties on though, I might need to get in some practice and I don't want to make you pink too soon.'

Carrie obliged, kept her bra and knickers on and leant over the pillows, facing down onto the airbed. She wobbled a bit as she tried to position herself. 'Whoa, this feels a bit like a waterbed,' she laughed. 'Nothing to do with all that whisky, of course.' She turned her head around to give Ian a provocative and enticing, if somewhat inebriated, look. 'I'm ready when you are, Daddy.'

He liked using the pillows. Apart from giving him ease of access, it pleased him the way the height accentuated the outline of her bum as it was raised in the air. He slapped her gently on her right cheek, just to remember the feel of it. They'd both been really busy at their respective jobs over the past few months and hadn't had a lot of time for their games. As a result, they'd promised each other this week of unadulterated sex and spanking. Ian smacked one buttock then the other with increasing force until he felt he'd got back into the groove again. He allowed a self-satisfied smile to escape as he lowered her panties so that they were resting behind her knees. He was turned on by that vulnerable look. Quickly, before Carrie had time to prepare for it, he gave her a resounding slap on her bare skin. He loved the way her flesh reverberated, and was followed by a glowing pinkness in the surrounding tissue. He felt a flame of heat travel down the length of his body and make its way to his swelling cock.

'Ouch!' It was out before she could stop herself. Carrie lowered her voice a fraction. 'That took me by surprise, you naughty man. Just as well our neighbours went to bed ages ago. Hopefully, they should be sleeping soundly by now.'

'They probably have their hearing aids switched off anyway and won't hear a thing. Which is just as well as I'm about to get started. And, by the way, I'm not the naughty one. You are, young lady.'

Ian knew what Carrie liked. He knew that she liked him to set up a rhythm and he began slowly, first one cheek and then the other. Carrie was responding with little whimpers that were growing in proportion to the force that Ian was exerting. He stopped for a minute, to get his breath, and to spread her legs wider so that he could watch the moisture shimmering, as she got wetter by the minute. He leant over and licked her inner thighs. She was beginning to pant loudly. He felt his cock straining even more against his boxer shorts.

'Where is it?' he asked.

'What?'

'You know what, don't tease.'

She waited until her breathing had calmed down, then said, 'In my washbag.'

Ian retrieved the hairbrush and held it so that the bristles were facing him. The frame was a smooth teak, the bristles natural – Boots's most expensive. He tapped her left cheek, gently at first, then a little stronger until he could see it reddening. With each slap of wood on skin, she emitted a guttural whimper. He repeated the process on her right buttock. Then lifted the brush to eye level, as though contemplating it.

'Oh, don't stop,' Carrie pleaded.

'Why not?' Ian teased.

'Oh, baby, don't stop now. Please. I'm coming soon, I can feel it.'

Ian loved it when she begged. 'Now for the other side,' he announced.

Carrie, becoming more and more breathless, was back in the game. 'Oh no, Daddy, not that. I promise I'll be good.'

'Oh, I know you'll be good, honey.' Ian twisted the brush in his fingers so that its long natural bristles were facing the skin of Carrie's buttocks. He brought it down until the sharp points were just pricking against her skin. Carrie was panting hard now in anticipation. The arc of his first swing was much wider than he'd planned and it hit Carrie with such force that she let out a loud scream. She immediately put her hand to her mouth.

'Oh, that hurt,' she gasped. Then she laughed. 'Not so strong, Daddy.'

'Oh, but you've been a naughty little girl, so naughty. This is what you deserve.' And he let the bristles fall again, although not so hard, just enough to invoke a desirous cry. He was aware that Carrie was approaching boiling point and he wanted to keep her simmering.

'Onto your back now,' he ordered. He knew this was the bit she liked best. He knew that when he got her to the right pitch – as she was now – by spanking her behind, she loved it even more when he turned his attention to her pussy. She was so breathless that she couldn't speak and her moaning had become quite voluble. She did as she was told and rolled onto her back without a word. Ian removed his boxers to allow Carrie to see his throbbing, stiff member, hard as steel and jutting out like a girder. She reached out to touch him, but he smiled and kept her at bay.

'This is your night,' he said. 'My turn tomorrow.' They gave each other a knowing grin.

The pillows, still beneath her, acted like a display stand for her glistening pussy. Ian spread her legs wide and held the brush over her. Then he brought it down gently and began using it to graze her pussy in long, languorous strokes. Carrie arched her back as though presenting herself to him, relaxing somewhat and enjoying the attention, but this wasn't what Ian wanted; he needed to keep her on edge. Despite her protestations, he put the brush away and, with an open hand, began to rhythmically tap her pussy, firstly with gentle little slaps. Then, as Carrie began to get more and more excited and started emitting groans that got louder and louder by the minute, Ian turned slightly so that he could cup his hand and create a kind of suction. With each tap, the pace got quicker, Carrie's grunts got louder, and Ian found himself responding just as noisily. The airbed whooshed up and down to their rhythm and, as he realised that Carrie was about to reach a resounding climax, Ian positioned himself over her body, and her cries of delight were quickly followed by his own.

The whole camping ground seemed to be awash with wailing sirens. That's possibly what woke everyone up – first the clamour, followed by the bright lights: blue, flashing lights like whirlpools of angry, luminous water. Children were whooping and screaming with excitement, babies were crying in fear, and adults were appraising the night attire of their fellow campers.

Carrie let out a moan; she was really very tired. She was still half asleep as she lifted herself up on her elbows, keeping her eyes closed against the brightness that was trying to penetrate her lids. She blindly felt around the airbed for Ian's body and when she found it she shook him soundly. He moaned. Carrie tried to speak but her voice was groggy, her throat dry. She coughed and managed to let out a croak.

'Please, Ian, you need to wake up, something's going on out there.' When there was still no response, she sat up more fully and opened her eyes – and looked straight into the face of a stern police officer. She screamed.

Ian, comatose next to her, moaned once more and then mumbled, 'Later, Carrie.'

The policeman coughed. 'I'm sorry to disturb you, madam, but we've received a complaint.'

Carrie shook her head, trying to understand. 'A complaint? What's it to do with us? What kind of complaint?' She really just wanted him to go away and leave them alone.

The officer stared at Ian as though willing him awake. 'Could you waken your husband, boyfriend, whatever, please? We need to have a word with him, with you both.'

'I'm trying, but he's out cold.' Carrie gave Ian a rough shake to prove her diagnosis and he immediately jumped up, alert.

'What? What is it? What's going on?'

The policeman removed his hat, coughing slightly while doing so, and indicated Ian's state of undress by ostentatiously looking away from him. Ian looked down and then quickly covered his erect penis.

Deeming it safe to return his gaze, the policeman looked back in Ian's direction and continued. 'Perhaps if you could both come outside, please? As soon as you're ready.' He backed out of the tent as though leaving royalty, although in reality there was no other way for him to get out.

When Ian and Carrie exited their tent, it was to a gathering crowd of curious onlookers. The motley group had formed a semi-circle around Carrie and Ian's tent and a collective intake of breath could be heard as the two stepped into view. Carrie held onto Ian's arm and positioned herself

31

behind him.

'All right, all right, the show's over,' the officer announced. He made shooing gestures but no one paid any attention. Having been so rudely awakened those gathered appeared in no hurry to return to their beds. From the safety of Ian's back, Carrie scanned the crowd, trying to ascertain what was going on. Some woman was passing out mugs of tea. Albert and Gladys were standing just to Carrie's left, looking concerned. Carrie tried to catch Gladys's attention but the old woman was determinedly avoiding eye contact. The policeman cleared his throat and addressed Carrie.

'Are you all right, madam?'

'Of course, I'm all right,' Carrie replied. 'Why shouldn't I be?' She wondered why all attention should fall on her well-being? Surely whatever had happened, the policeman should be more concerned with the young children, or with women on their own. Why her?

The officer moved in closer, in an attempt to keep their conversation semi-private. 'Well, we've had a complaint, madam,' he repeated. 'Someone called in and said that they thought you were being assaulted.' He coughed again, looking somewhat embarrassed. 'Has this man assaulted you?' he asked. 'You can safely tell us. He won't be able to harm you again.' He bobbed his head to the right and left as he spoke, as though trying to get a good look at Carrie. At any minute she expected him to shine his torch on her face. And then she suddenly understood what it was all about and with that awareness came the amusing realisation that it wasn't her face he would need to shine the torch on. She tried not to snigger. She nudged Ian and whispered to the back of his head.

'It's about our game. What are we going to do?'

Ian appeared just as defeated. 'Don't know,' he murmured back to her through clenched teeth. He turned his head to whisper in her ear. 'I think we'll have to explain, otherwise I'm going to get arrested.'

Ian stepped away from Carrie and emitted his own version of an embarrassed cough.

'Em, excuse me, constable, I think there's been a misunderstanding. If I could have a word with you in private, sir?' He realised that he was sounding rather pathetically sycophantic. He motioned for the police officer to follow him behind their tent. The policeman hesitated at first, checked that his partner was aware of the situation and then followed Ian into the darkness, out of the reach of the bright flashing arcs.

They were gone for several minutes, leaving Carrie alone to face the crowd. She felt like a circus act. Most people were huddled in groups, and in between bouts of chatter, would turn to look in her direction. Carrie caught Albert's eye, but he immediately glanced away. Gladys, however, now sent Carrie a sympathetic look and sidled up to her.

'I'm sorry,' she said quietly, 'but I thought he was hurting you.'

Carried drew in her breath. 'You?' she shouted accusingly, then lowered her voice when it began to attract an audience. Gladys offered an apologetic smile then looked as if she was going to burst into tears. Carrie took pity on her and turned them both away from the encroaching curiosity. 'It's OK,' she said, 'don't worry about it. I'm sure Ian will sort it out.' She looked back towards the other campers to make sure no one was eavesdropping. 'It's just a game Ian and I play; it's fun. Sometimes it just gets out of hand.' She laughed inwardly at her own witticism. 'We sometimes get carried away, if you know what I mean.' Actually, she wasn't sure that Gladys did know what she meant, and was about to move back to her tent, when she felt Gladys's hand on her arm, stopping her.

'Doesn't it hurt?' she whispered anxiously.

Carrie let out a quiet guffaw. 'The first spank takes you by surprise,' she confided, 'but then it becomes quite thrilling. I can't really explain it. The hairbrush stings a little bit at first, but it's an electrifying tingle.' Carrie stopped. From the look she was getting from Gladys, she surmised that was a tad too much information. 'Anyway, I'm sorry we woke you up.'

Gladys patted her arm. 'And I'm sorry I got you into this trouble.' Before they could say any more, Ian and the police officer returned from their sojourn behind the tent, their faces red but with a look of relief on them.

'OK, OK, it's all sorted now. It's all just a mistake, nothing to concern anyone. Now, back to your beds, folks.'

The officer made some ineffective shooing motions once more, then he replaced his hat, signalled for the ambulance to leave, and headed for his car. The lights, which had been flashing throughout, were switched off and the campers reluctantly returned to their tents and caravans, disappointedly deprived of a show.

The following morning, Ian and Carrie had their tent down and their things packed in the car long before the rest of the campers were up and about.

'We'll get breakfast in the next village,' Ian assured Carrie. 'Let's just get away from here ASAP.' Carrie quietly nodded her agreement. She was just about to sit down on the pillow that was lining the passenger seat, and Ian was already at the wheel, revving up, ready to go, when they saw Gladys emerge from her tent. She walked across to the blue Peugeot that was parked alongside their tent and flipped the switch to unlock it. Then she leant inside and removed something from the glove compartment. Ian found reverse gear and backed out of their parking space, leaving a patch of flattened grass where their own tent had been.

Carrie watched Gladys lock her car again, but before she re-entered her tent, the old woman turned to wave goodbye to the couple. Something sparkled in the early sunlight; it was a silver-backed hairbrush, shining in Gladys's hand.

The Uninitiated Bottom
by D L King

'Haven't you ever wondered about bottoming?'

That's how the whole thing started. I'd gone for breakfast with Frank and his boy after a long night of playing at one of our favourite clubs.

A night of play burns a lot of calories and I'm always too wired to just go home and go to bed. I have to eat and relax – process the night, and it's great to be able to do that with Frank. Frank's been my friend and mentor since I entered the scene. We're both tops and we both prefer to play with boys. That pretty much makes Frank gay and me straight, and like I said, we've been friends for years; we obviously have the same interests, we're both dominants and we get along great.

I took a sip of coffee and mulled it over. 'Yeah, maybe, but not really,' I said. 'I don't know. I'm just not a bottom. Not really into pain and humiliation – well, not unless I'm the one dealing it. Frank, you know me. Can you imagine me saying "yes, sir" and doing what I'm told?'

'I don't see how you can top someone if you've never bottomed.' Frank's partner, Marty, is both intelligent and adorable. He's the "boy" to Frank's "sir" in the relationship, but once they step out of scene, he doesn't hang back. He's an equal partner who speaks his mind.

'Yeah,' I said, 'I've heard that before, but I don't buy it.' Our eggs came, and the smell of bacon was intoxicating. I let my brain stop functioning for a minute while I took a bite. It hit the spot.

'I could probably go through the motions, but why? It's not like I don't know what stuff feels like, at least as much as I can – not being a guy. I always try new things on myself before playing with them. It's like I said, pain doesn't turn me on. And Marty, seriously, can you imagine me being all subby?'

'So, you're telling me there's nothing you're curious about – nothing you like having done to you?' Frank asked.

'I don't know,' I replied. 'I mean, sometimes I like being flogged and sometimes I like being bound. But it's always at my direction. You know me: I'm a control freak.'

'What, and I'm not?' Marty piped up. Frank laughed that laugh that was part chuckle and part growl and gave him a kiss.

'I'm just saying, I'm not a sub. I'm not the "defer to others" kind. Why? You ever bottomed, Frank?'

'Sure,' Frank said. 'Back when I got into the scene, you had to bottom to top.'

A brief picture of Frank, naked in some leatherman's dungeon flashed through my mind. I wondered what that had been like for him – what it might have been like for me – and then we got busy eating and talking about other things. The topic of my bottoming was dismissed in favour of a second cup of coffee and another order of hash browns. Afterward, we headed to our respective homes, hopefully to get to bed before the sun came up.

For once, the trains cooperated and I made it home in record time but, for some reason, I was too restless to sleep. I couldn't turn off my brain. My mind replayed the evening's play and occasionally mixed in the breakfast conversation. Some weird fantasy of bottoming to Frank was becoming attractive, and I didn't want to know why. It was probably that second cup of coffee. The damn birds got really loud at first light, but calmed down after a while and I was able to fall asleep.

Although I hadn't forgotten our conversation, and occasionally the idea of my submitting began to look slightly intriguing, that train of thought fell to the backburner until a couple of weeks later when Frank called to invite me to dinner. Marty's a trained chef, so I never pass up an opportunity to eat at their house.

I rang the bell and Frank answered, wearing jeans, a T-shirt and a black apron, holding a spatula. 'Hey. Come on in,' he said.

The first thing that crossed my mind was that Frank looked kind of hot and commanding in the black apron, but then I snapped out of it. 'What's the deal?' I asked, following him through the house to the backyard.

'What do you mean?'

'Where's Marty? What's with the apron?'

'Oh! Yeah, Marty's working tonight. It's just you and me. I thought I'd barbecue. Grab a beer. You want cheese on your burger?'

'Yeah, sure.' I got a beer from the fridge and yelled, 'You want one?'

'No, I'm good.'

Following the scent of roasting meat, I went back outside. 'Geez, man; if I'd known that Marty wasn't cooking, I'd have opted for another night. I'm sure you make a perfectly adequate hamburger and everything ...' I added, grinning at him.

'I'm burning your cheese,' he said. 'On purpose.'

The burgers turned out to be great, the beer was cold and the day was about as serenely suburban as they come. Once we were both satiated and I was well into my second beer, Frank said, 'I wanted to talk to you about bottoming to me.' Just like that. No preamble – nothing.

'What? Why would I want to do that? Why would *you* want to do that?'

Frank looked at me; held me with an intense gaze.

'Because I think it's important.' He blinked and smiled. 'And because we're friends and we trust each other.'

Of course Frank didn't know I'd been thinking about this off and on – maybe more on than off – since that night. I think I might have brought it up if he hadn't.

'We'll pick a day when Marty's working,' he continued. 'He doesn't have to be involved or even know anything about this if you don't want him to, but I think it's something you should experience – something you need to understand.'

And that's how I wound up naked, in Frank's dungeon a week later.

I'd been there plenty of times. He'd taught me there. He'd watched me take charge of my first real scene there. We'd topped guys together there; we'd even topped Marty together there. This was the first time I'd ever been naked there – or naked in front of Frank anywhere, for that matter. But after all, this was Frank. I trusted Frank like I trusted myself. Maybe I didn't have any idea why I'd said yes, but it just seemed like the natural thing to do.

We walked into the dungeon together, as equals, but as soon as the door closed, he ordered me to strip. I just looked at him. Of course I'd known this was coming, it made me slightly nauseous but also initiated a bit of a tingle – I didn't know how to react.

He said it again: 'Strip.'

'OK.'

He slapped my face. Not hard, really. Just to get my attention. 'What did you say?'

I smiled; couldn't help it. 'Geez, Frank, I said OK.'

'You will call me "sir". That's my name in here. You will say "yes, sir" or "no, sir" when I ask you a question. That's all you'll say. You will do what I tell you to do when I tell you to do it. Is that clear?'

I studied him for a second. He was completely in dom mode – every inch the consummate leatherman. His short-sleeved, faded, blue cotton workshirt showed off the muscles in his arms. It was tucked into tight, well-worn, black leather pants, topped off with a black leather belt and engineer boots. I could easily see what his boys saw in him, but he was still Frank to me – my mentor and friend. 'Yes, sir,' I said. I began to wonder if I looked that impressive to my boys as I slowly began to take off my clothes.

'I haven't got all day, girl. Hurry it up.'

'Yes, sir,' I said and quickly removed the last bit of underwear.

'Face me and stand up straight. Do you agree to wear my collar today?'

I nodded my head.

'Say it. I want to hear you say you agree.'

'Yes, sir, I agree to wear your collar while we play today.' As he buckled the leather around my neck, I shivered and wondered if this was what it was like for my boys, when I collared them for play. That sort of got me thinking specifically about Tom, my current sub, and how he might feel when I ordered him to get naked. Which started me thinking about our next play date and how I might want to start it off – flogging against the cross or spanking on the horse ... He had a really nice ass ...

The next thing I knew, I was getting smacked in the face again, not quite as gently as the last time. It snapped my focus back to Frank and the situation at hand.

'Laura!'

I realised I was now wearing ankle and wrist cuffs, as well as the collar. 'Sorry,' I said. 'I'm sorry. I was thinking about ...'

Frank glared. Grabbed a nipple and twisted. 'Sir!'

'Sir,' I yelped. 'I'm sorry, sir!'

He caught my eye and held my attention while he pinched my nipple harder. 'I don't care what you were thinking about.' He slapped me again, and then again, checking to be sure he had my attention. I saw his hand come up again and I raised my arm to block the next slap. He grabbed my wrist, then my other wrist and held them up, over my head. With his face about six inches from mine, he gave me a menacing look. 'Don't you dare. In here, you're mine to do with as I please.'

The safe word we'd discussed previously – "pineapple" – passed through my mind and was quickly dismissed. What kind of wuss would I be, ending this scene before it even got started? But I hated being slapped in the face more than anything. I couldn't remember; had we ever discussed that? He was pushing my buttons.

He pressed my wrists against the wall, on either side of my face, and then removed his hands. I kept mine where he'd placed them. Backing up a bit, he slapped me until my cheek was burning. I felt my anger build – and then I felt something else; something I almost didn't recognise. It was a little like resignation, but not really that. Actually, it was almost a feeling of tranquillity.

Frank clipped my wrists about shoulder-height to eyebolts in the wall and slowly pinched both my nipples, applying more and more pressure until I moaned. His ensuing face-slap felt like punctuation – like the period at the end of a sentence.

'Pick up your foot,' he said. And when I did, he moved it a little to the left and clipped the ankle cuff to what must have been another eyebolt in the wall. He moved my other foot further to the right, stretching my legs uncomfortably wide, and clipped that ankle to the wall as well before stepping back for an appraising look. 'You're smaller than most of the boys I play with, so you'll probably be a little more uncomfortable, but it'll have to do.'

He went back to slapping my face again, this time a little more gently, but now he was punishing both sides of my face. I'd started out staring at him, but slowly my eyes began to close. It was probably in response to the sight of his hands too close to my eyes, but after they were closed for a while, I could sense a change. It was almost like a drift of consciousness.

'You like that, don't you,' he asked.

Had I been smiling? I opened my eyes. 'No.'

'I think you *do* like it.'

'I hate it,' I retorted.

He reached down, between my legs, and ran his fingers through my slit. I was slick with moisture. He brought them up to my nose and said, 'I beg to differ.' He wiped his fingers off on my upper lip. 'Oh, you're so easy.' He laughed. 'It won't be long before I have you begging.'

Yeah, I doubted it. This was becoming a contest of wills. Was he forgetting I was a domme? A lot of thoughts ran through my head: *Easy? I'll give him easy*; *He'll never make me beg*; *Is this really turning me on?*; *What if I'm really a bottom?*; *I'm just playing along – this means nothing to me*; *Fuck him, if he thinks he can just keep slapping me*; *Beg, my ass*.

He caught my expression and my little smile and said, 'You're in the dark now – you have no idea. In fact, I think I'll keep you in the dark. It'll be good for you.' While he continued to stare me in the eye, he reached for something hanging against the wall and then fastened the black rubber blindfold around my face. Very thin, it was completely opaque and moulded easily to the contours of my face. My breathing sped a little and the scent of the rubber mixed with the scent of my arousal to form something completely different.

'No.'

'No what?'

'No blindfold.' I shook my head from side to side.

'No blindfold what?'

I thought for a second. What? Oh. 'No blindfold, *sir*. I don't like the blindfold.' Being deprived of sight felt like losing control and I fought it.

'That's OK; *I* like it.' He planted a kiss on my nose.

I thought about pineapple juice. I thought about pineapple rings on ham. I even thought about piña coladas, but I didn't say anything. Losing my sight disturbed me more than I ever thought it would. I felt like I was shrinking.

I heard some clinking, rattling noises, and then felt a sharp stab of pain in my nipple, quickly followed by the same sensation in the other one. I think I screeched, but I'm not sure it was out loud. There was a heavy metal chain connecting the nipple clamps and it swung against my body. A disconnected thought ran through my brain – of course, he plays with boys – he uses heavy toys. The combined weight of the clamps and the chain pulled my nipples downward, adding to the pain.

Nothing else touched me. Was he giving me a moment to get used to the clamps or was he preparing something else? My senses reached out to try to figure out where he was – what his next move would be. I tried to imagine what he was doing so I could prepare for it – what would I do, if it was me, if this was my scene? I jumped when I felt his hand fingering my cunt lips, but before I could relax into the feeling, I felt twin stabs of pain as similar clamps were affixed to my labia.

'I usually use those on a boy's sac. They don't look half-bad on you.' I heard a deep, masculine chuckle. 'Of course I usually weight them ...' I heard scrabbling noises and then felt the clamps dig in deep as they were pulled down by the weights he hung. 'Interesting effect. Does it feel nice?' I think I whimpered – or maybe I didn't make any noise at all.

I felt the rush of air before I felt the slap against my cheek. It woke up my stinging face. 'Answer me.'

'Um–'

The face slapping was renewed. 'Answer me. Does it feel good? Do you like it?' Each sentence was punctuated with a slap.

'Yes. No. I don't know,' I wailed.

The rhythm of his slaps was a constant. 'What?'

'I don't know, I don't know. Sir! I said, sir – I meant sir – I said – I don't know.' My body emitted a low animal sound. It was the embodiment of frustration, of surrender – of pleasure. 'Yes, yes, OK? Yes, it feels good,' I moaned, swinging my hips forward. The motion caused the weights to swing, pulling on my lips more and I groaned.

He ran his fingers through the open gash of my sex and I felt them slide inside. I'd never felt so open before. When he removed them I whimpered again. 'No, no, no, no,' I pleaded even as he brought them up to my nose and lips. He spread the slick juices on my lips, forcing his fingers inside my mouth and I sucked on them.

As I sucked, tasting the flavour of my arousal, I felt new bright flashes of pain in my nipples as he pulled and twisted the chain connecting those clamps and I moaned and rocked my body forward, toward his tormenting hands.

He dropped the chain to let it bounce against my chest again and ran his fingers slowly down my torso to my swollen pussy. His fingers played on the wet insides of my labia, dipping into my open cunt and back out. They circled my throbbing clit, never touching the ache. I moaned and groaned, pushing myself toward the hand, making the weights bounce and swing but he made sure to stay out of range of the point of pleasure he knew I sought.

'You want to come? You want me to make you come?'

I groaned and nodded.

'Say it. Tell me you want to come. *Beg* me to let you come.'

'Please,' I groaned. 'Please, sir, please make me come,' I said. 'Do it,' I yelled. 'Please ...' He continued to finger me, fucking my opening and pulling on the chain, tightening the labial clamps. 'Yes, yes, please do it. Please make me come. Please, pleasepleaseplease,' I begged

I felt a searing pain in my clit as he pinched it and, at the same time, buried his finger deep inside me, scraping against my g-spot as he went. The vibration started in my

43

toes and shot up my legs as a similar vibration centred in my nipples, gripped my breasts and shot down my torso. The orgasm taking hold of my cunt was answered in my head, as I felt the electricity flow over my stinging face, through my fingers and dance on my clit. I threw my head back and screamed my pleasure. It seemed to go on and on, building on itself, until finally I hung limply against the wall as the last few tremors shook me.

I felt the back of Frank's hand caress my cheek and then he removed the blindfold. I blinked in the light of the dungeon and then closed my eyes.

'Get ready for it,' he said as I felt his hands go to the clamps on my nipples. I winced as he removed them and then bathed the sore, red nubs of flesh with his tongue. He gently squeezed my breasts and the nipples, helping to get the circulation going again and normalize the feeling. 'Better?' he asked.

'Yes, thanks.'

'How you doin'?'

'Fine,' I replied automatically.

'Mm hm,' he said, as he removed the weights from the chain attached to the labial clamps. 'It's OK, you're safe. I gotcha. Ready?' He removed both clamps and grabbed me between the legs and squeezed as an involuntary shiver coursed through my body with the ensuing orgasm.

'Mmm, I think I love you.' It was a kind of involuntary bedroom voice. After my body settled I hurried to add, 'But don't slap my face again.'

Frank laughed as he bent down to unfasten the clips on my ankle cuffs. I slowly brought my legs together to begin to relieve the cramping from the strained pose while he hugged me to him and unhooked my wrists. 'That's right, I gotcha,' he said again as I slumped into his arms. He walked me over to a leather-covered bench and sat me down, my back leaning against the wall. He handed me a glass of water and sat with me until I asked for my clothes.

'You OK now?'

'Yeah, I'm good,' I said.

'All right, want to get dressed and come upstairs? Marty prepared a nice dinner for us. All I have to do is put it in the oven. He said he left foolproof instructions. He thought you'd probably deserve a good meal after your "ordeal". I'll put out some cheese and crackers and open a bottle of wine and we can talk.'

I told Frank that all sounded great. After he left, I sat back to get comfortable in my skin. I'd just pleaded with a man to be allowed to come. I guess there truly is a first time for everything. A shiver ran up my spine. I knew the experience wasn't going to change who or what I was, but it definitely gave me some things to think about. I found I couldn't wait to discuss it all with Frank – find out what bottoming had been like for him – compare notes. I got dressed and headed upstairs. Time to replace those burnt calories.

Split
by Shanna Germain

Every time Prose comes back to me, she brings something new. Last time it was thigh-high stockings, black, with little ribbons at the top to hold them up. She sat in my chair and watched while I pulled them off her with my teeth, revelling in each revealed expanse of her pale flesh, the sun-brined taste of her after so long away.

Without saying a word of hello, she tied one of the stockings around my mouth, so that every time I breathed, all I could taste was her skin. When she spread her thighs, she put one newly exposed foot on my chest, held me away from her while she dipped her red-tipped fingers between her glistening lips. With every stroke, the smell of her – mint and wet earth and the shifting sea – rose against my nose and I trembled and squirmed before her. She never let me touch her, not even as she was gasping and moaning my name, not even as she bucked her hips in my chair a thousand times. Not even when I begged on my knees before her.

The time before that, it was a long black whip. And lessons – she'd learnt to wield the weapon while she'd been gone, and it snaked from her hand with a sharp coil before it landed, so soft, to stroke against my back. Soft, but only the first time. After that, after that night with her flickering strokes against my skin, I could barely work. Every fabric shift against my back pulled my breath tight, made me fight to bury a groan of pain in my throat. I'm the boss here; it wouldn't do to let the minions see me in agony, and so I bore it silently, gritting my teeth. But she knew. Oh, how she knew what it did to me, even as she ran her fingertips over the healing wounds, spreading oils along the broken skin.

I don't know where she gets the means for these things. I don't ask. If I did, she would likely say it was from selling her paintings, but I know for a fact that she doesn't sell them. She gives them away. It's the one soft side of her.

I never know when she's going to be done painting the world toward winter so she can come back to me. She's due any day, since the word from the new arrivals is that the leaves have tipped, yellow and gold with envy, and that her mother is already stalking the cities, her hair pulled into a bun so tight that it makes her look permanently pissed off.

I sleep and eat and work, but fitfully, sure that every sound is the one that precedes Prose's arrival. I begin to think that she has forgotten me, that she will not come this year. 'Deals are deals until they aren't,' is what my brother always says, and I wonder now if she thinks the same thing. If she's changed her mind and found a way to break herself free of obligation. She's that kind of woman. Hard to pin down. Hard to force.

Everything above turns to white skies and ice – this is what the hordes say – and still she does not come.

I pace, striding and glowering. Barking orders. Everyone expects this kind of attitude from me, yet I can't help but feel that they're laughing at me behind my back. That they know the reason behind my temper. They know better than to show their laughter to me. I handle a whip as well as she does, better even, and I make it clear that I can dish up far worse punishments than a stroke of leather. Punishments that last an eternity.

Finally, I retreat to my private floor, winding my way through the rooms, picking up things and setting them down.

'Pater? Why are you pacing?' It's her voice behind me and I'd been so distracted by my thoughts of her I didn't hear her arrive. I turn, and there she is: that glorious flow of red hair, so thick and dark it's nearly purpled. Her lips tinted to match, the edges of them fluttering as she tries to keep them from curling. The tiny, blood-red jewel that glitters at her throat. I'd forgotten how perfectly it fits the lean curve of her neck. The outfit is new, as it always is when she returns. This time it's a skin-tight pomegranate-hued dress, some shiny material that shows off every curve and ends abruptly just above her knees. A bit of pale dimpled knee shows, and then the rest of her leg is captured by black boots, made of the same material.

I have to catch my breath, not just from the sheer glory of her after so long away, but also to keep myself from crying out, from going down on my knees in front of her hems and bawling like a baby, 'Where have you been?'

Instead, I swallow back my desires and drop my chin near my chest, eyes down. My cock has hardened at the mere sight of her – it pushes against its fabric confines, aching for release. My exhale – I know she can hear it too – is of a man who's waited far too long for his punishment and is now relieved that it's finally arrived.

'I heard ...' She takes a single step forward, those boots somehow silent despite the tall heels. She always did move like the moon, silent through whatever sky she decided to occupy. At the moment, I'm just grateful it's my sky she's wandering through. 'I heard you had a little ... mmm ... how shall I put this? Conquest?'

'No,' I say. Simple and plain, but there is a heartbeat of fear in my words, and I know she can hear it.

'No?'

'It was ... I was ...' The girl was so green and fresh, I want to say. She reminded me of you, ages ago. But I don't say this. Of course I don't.

She steps forward, closing the space between us until I

49

can smell her. The coal and fire scent of work, of this place, recedes, is replaced by the smell of her hair. Her curls carry the wind and spice of autumn and the scent swirls around me until I'm light-headed.

'Ah, poor boy, grovelling for forgiveness already? I'd have expected more from someone as strong as yourself.' One of her hands is behind her back and the other reaches forward, a single fingernail lifting my chin with its slow furrow beneath my throat. 'Someone who rules a place like this ...'

As she taunts me, a flash of hot anger clenches my fists tight. I force myself to pull it together, to stand strong in front of her, settling my gaze on those darkened eyes of hers.

'Nothing happened,' I say, and a thousand clichés fill my mouth, but I don't let them fall out.

'Hmph. I talked to the bitch already, Pater.' Her hand slides into my hair, clenches at the side of it, and begins to push me down in front of her. 'I've ... stamped her out already, oh yes.' My knees give, and I buckle before her, my head just at the height of her plasticky hem. I can smell her already, although the scent of her is contaminated by the material she wears.

'You didn't,' I say. Not that I care for the girl, particularly, but I know how Prose is, once she gets something in her mind. I whisper, but I have to say it. 'She was just a girl.'

'And now she is no longer,' Prose says. Her voice is frosty, and I wonder yet again why she paints in greens and yellows instead of with the cold blues and dead whites of winter.

'And look what I brought for you, Pater,' she says in a purr, as though she's never been away. As though she didn't just question my loyalty, my fidelity. As though she didn't just admit to wiping out a young green goddess with nothing more than jealousy.

From behind her back, she brings forth a long thin box. The kind of box that only bears roses or death. I am not sure which I'd rather have from her.

There is a kind of sadness in her voice as she pulls off the lid, lets it fall down beside me. 'Not that such bad boys deserve gifts ... but I can hardly resist you, even when you've pissed me off.'

I can't see what's in the box, but my back is already tightening at the thought of it. Another whip? In the mood she's in, I hope not. A crop? Likely. A knife? It wouldn't be the first time.

The thing she pulls out as she lets the box drop away, the cardboard thudding down beside me, is thick and long and black. But not whip nor crop nor knife. I can see even from here that it's a cock. Twice as big around as my own – and I'm built like a god – the impossible length of it in her hand, the head curled and rising at the end like a fist. I can't imagine where she got it, who stood in place to mould such a thing; my mind reels with images of bulls and horses. My own throat clenches involuntarily at the sight of it. My cock, on the other hand, arches against the fabric so hard that I'm afraid the material will rip apart.

'Skirt up, Pater,' she says, stroking the black beast in her hand more lovingly than she's ever stroked mine.

I reach up with both hands, fumbling for the skirt's hem, sliding it upward over her pale smooth thighs. My fingers tremble against her skin, and I try to quell their shake by pressing my palms hard against her as the skirt reveals the top of her thighs and then, finally, gloriously, the dark red coils of hair that triangle between her legs. Woven in some intricate pattern that my mind cannot comprehend at the moment is a black leather harness, thin strips that coil around her hips and between her legs. I nearly forget her anger, nearly forget the cock that she's holding, my tongue aching for the taste of her, and I lean in, my knees against the hard floor, to sink my mouth against those damp curls.

Her hand tightens in my hair in a flash, pulling me away so hard I see swirls of pain in front of my eyes.

'No, no,' she says, like I'm nothing more than a creature to be beaten upon the ground at her feet. And perhaps I'm not. Maybe I wanted her angry, maybe that's why I kissed the little nymph girl. To see if she'd hear about it and come charging back. Maybe this time to stay for good.

She lets go of my head and takes a step backward, adjusting the straps to slide the black cock into its place between her thighs. At this level, right in front of my face, it's huge. Impossibly huge. I can already imagine its taste between my teeth, the swelling bulk of the head pressing into the back of my throat. The sound of my broken groan mimics the rhythm that beats against my neck, the same one that pulses inside the length of my cock.

Stroking it slowly, as though it's her own, she leans her upper body back, jutting her hips out toward me. 'Eat from me, Pater,' she says. 'Eat me the way I once ate from you, so very long ago.'

I can't resist, even though I know what it's going to feel like going in. I can smell how it will taste, rubbery and thick, choking me. I rest my lips to the thick head, feel her roll her hips against me, seeking entrance. All it takes is a parting of my lips and she's forcing her new cock down, between my teeth, and I realise it doesn't matter if my teeth are clenched. It's just rubber, after all. Biting down would do nothing in my favour. So I give way, open up to her forward thrusts.

The cock fills my mouth so completely that I can't breathe. I've forgotten that I can use my nose and I merely hold my breath, head swimming, until she chooses to pull back. I cough and gasp at the air that flows back in, catching a quick breath before she plunges forward again. This time, she grips both hands on either side of my head, tugging my mouth over her length. It nudged against my throat and I gag against the taste of rubber, the dull press of the rounded head against my reflex.

'Get it wet,' she husks, voice choked with lust. It's a sound that makes my muscles hum, my already strained senses begin to implode, one by one. If I could look down and see myself around her huge erection, I know I'd be staining the fabric.

'Very wet,' she adds. 'Because you know,' each word punctuated by a sharp thrust of her hips. 'Where. It's. Going.' Even around my gagging, choking hold of her cock, I know she means to put this thing inside me, to bury it deep between my cheeks. The very thought of it makes my ass clench, a violent shudder of fear and want that slides up through me.

'Good boy.' The cock doesn't impede my groan as her words start another small tremor through my stomach, my hips. She strokes my hair with one hand, the other curled hard at the back of my neck to keep pulling me against her, sinking the entire cock into my mouth and throat, mashing my face into her dark curls each time she's hilted inside me. She's close to coming; I can tell by the scent of her – musky as dying flowers – and by the way she speeds up her thrusts, the movements turning wild and feral. 'Such a good boy, aren't you, my king?'

I want nothing more in that moment than to please her, than to bury every part of her inside the slick heat of my mouth. To feel her come against my lips, to feel her pulsed orgasm slide down the rubber cock, vibrate against my tongue and throat.

She pulls away, slides the entire length of the cock out of my mouth at the same time she digs her hands into my hair, holding me still. The cockhead barely rests against my lips, glistening and pulsing lightly.

Growling, I lean in. I can't help it. I want it back inside me. To fill me again. She's got me caught, fingers and nails, and I can't reach. I haven't made her come, and right now, I want nothing more than that. Of course she knows it. She tilts my head back so that I can see her face, past the shiny blackness, and her expression is one of barely holding on, of a dark delight. I wonder how much effort it took her to pull away without coming. If I licked her, just once, put the tip of my tongue against the dark red seed between her lips, I know she'd come. She's that close.

But I can't. I won't. I'm hers to do with as she will, and she knows it.

'Get undressed,' she says, one hand stroking her cock, slowly and carefully, as though she too is afraid she might come before her games with me are finished. 'And get on your hands and knees. I want to spank your ass while I fuck you.'

I drop my chin, unable to resist a soft groan. And I strip myself for her, in front of her, without once looking up. My knees already ache from resting on the hard floor, but it is a good ache, and I go down again, my back to her this time, my palms flat, making a bridge of my body for her, the kind that she uses to get from the world above to my domain below.

My full hard cock sways like a pendulum, counting the minutes, the hours that she is here with me. I am dripping on the floor, the sweat and moisture rolling off my tip to splatter lightly beneath me.

I hear her move behind me, the purposeful click-click of her heels as she bends down and touches a few fingers to the head of my cock, swirling through the moisture. From the side, she draws her fingers across my lips, coating my mouth with her own heat and the sulphur-stained taste of my body. I suck the digits ravenously. I've never been so hungry, so greedy. She pulls away too soon.

She stands, and the sound of ripping fabric makes me turn my head, but she forces it back forward with a single push of her boot.

'Forehead down,' she says.

I do as she asks, sinking my forehead to the floor. The

54

movement causes my ass to rise, and I shiver. Exposed before her. The fabric wraps my head, cuts across the corners of my lips so that every time I breathe, I get our mingled scents inside my mouth. Another piece slides beneath my hips, tightens like a noose.

She drags her fingers lightly between the crook of my ass, smearing my skin with something. Grease? Oil? I don't know. Only that I welcome the slow intrusion of her fingers, doing all I cannot to push back over them. I try not to think about the cock that she's wearing, the sheer size of it, the mushroom head that will split me open.

But then she's pushing the head against me, and I can think of nothing else. I am being shoved open, broken and torn. And I want it. I am ashamed to admit how I want it.

'Oh ... fuck ...' My voice is more groan than words, muffled to the ground.

'Just be glad ...' She slides in a bit more, a burning pleasure that rises up through my hips and cock. 'That I lubed you up first. Next time I'm shoving it straight in.'

I know she wouldn't. Of course she wouldn't. She's an iron queen, but she's not a cruel one. Not most of the time.

When her hand comes down on me, it's a shock. The tingled pain beneath the sound of the smack. But it's also a relief. The sting against my skin takes away from the dark burn that's opening my ass with each of her slow rolls into me.

She fills me and fills me and every time I think there is no more to be taken, nor any way for me to take any more, she opens me up just enough to sink farther. Until the tip is ramming against the spot inside that makes me writhe beneath her, back my ass into her oncoming strokes, beg her for more. One hand holds the fabric around my waist, pulling me backwards with each thrust. The other works my skin in sharp slaps, creating a pattern of her own design across my ass.

Her breath falls harsh and ragged, and I know this time

she won't be able to stop. She'll have to come. The very thought makes my own orgasm rise to a near boil, threatening to spill over.

She feels it and fucks me hard, panting her words, the sound dark with delight. 'Going to come for me, Pater?' she asks. Even as my name slides out of her lips, I can hear the groan of her orgasm rising, rising, planting itself into me with each thrust of her cock.

'Yes,' I hiss in answer, teeth clenched around the sharp release that starts against the tip of her cock, sparks outward through my hips and out through my cock, sending my hot seed spurting.

'Good boy,' she croons in a choked gasp as she continues to come behind me and inside me, forcing my own orgasm through me until I am filled with nothing but her – her name, her scent, her cock, her coming. I groan her name, over and over, until my voice is nothing but a growled song to her.

'Mmm, I've missed you, Pater,' she says, as she begins to ever so slowly pull her cock out of me, a hand softly brushing the marks on my skin.

I know it's true. And I hope that this time she will decide to stay.

Acting Tough
by Landon Dixon

I plucked up the latest issue of my favourite pulp, *Dan Turner, Hollywood Detective*, leafed through the turgid contents. I barked out a chuckle, eyeballing the froth and frolic. That Dan Turner, he knew just how to work a case. I needed a case to work.

The Depression wasn't just a financial reality any more, it was a state of mind – mine. The soles of my shoes had more holes than FDR's NRA, and I had less money to fill them in. Hollywood was still shining bright, but yours truly was a reel away from fade to black.

Some yob bumped me. I slotted the pulp, spun. 'Watch where you're sticking your wingtip, pal,' I snarled.

Then I pulled my tongue up short, recognising the gaucho standing in front of that newsstand at Hollywood and Vine. Mack Taylor, he-man star of the Rancho Pictures westerns, all 145 of them so far.

He was even bigger and broader off the screen and his horse and in person. Deep-set blue eyes in a chiselled, sunbrowned face sporting a prow of granite, short blond hair rustling in the dry Santa Ana winds, shoulders straining the cross-stitching on a spangled shirt, thighs flaring a pair of jeans to the point of blocking out the sun between his legs. The only thing this moving picture was missing was a 20-gallon hat and a pair of shit-kicking cowboy boots.

'Hey, you're–'

'I know who I am,' the celluloid cowpoke drawled. 'You too. You're a dick, right? A snoop?'

I liked his looks, but not his attitude. 'Yeah, I'm a PI. So what? Need someone to find the horse you rode in on?'

He shoved me back into the shelves of pulps, hard. Manny looked up from the half-naked picture of Stanwyck he'd been drooling over. 'Hey, boys, you wanna play, take it 'round the alley in back.'

'Fine with me,' Taylor grunted.

'Let's go, Tex,' I growled. 'You're one bronc I'm gonna enjoy bustin'.'

He took a swing at my konk as soon as we went from lightness to dark, into the alley. I ducked, handed him back a snootful of balled knuckles. It seemed a shame to mess up a pan like that, but I wasn't his make-up artist.

Taylor bounced off the opposite wall and down to his knees. He didn't get up. He grabbed onto my ankles, started kissing my feet.

'Sweet tumblin' tumbleweeds,' I rasped, looking down at the macho man making love to my Florsheims.

'I'm sorry. I submit. I'll do anything you want,' he whimpered.

I hadn't seen a guy fold like that since Schmeling–Louis II. He was actually buffing my dog-muffs with his tongue, swirling his wet pink mouth-noodle all around the polished patent leather.

'What's your problem, Taylor?' I gritted. 'Real life too different than reel life for you?'

He only whimpered some more, herded his big hands all around my calves, swabbing my shoes with his tongue. And then his mitts shot up my pant legs, and he looked up at me with pleading want in his big blue glims.

It struck me then, square in the groin, where a man does most of his good thinking – big, tough, rugged Mack Taylor was a submissive, as compliant as a bridled sheep once you showed him who was boss. He was also gayer than a Busby

58

Berkeley show-stopper. I deduced that steamy nugget when the guy's palms moseyed right up my legs to join forces at my groin.

'Whoa there, cowboy,' I said, reining in the back-alley rodeo. 'I need lettuce, not lovin'. You got a case for me to crack, or what?'

He nodded, desperately.

I shot a glance at the mouth of the alley – it was as empty as my wallet. I cast my gander the opposite way – the alley ran blind, up against a brick wall, no one else in sight.

'Lick my shoes, you pathetic bum,' I commanded.

Mack made with the tongue-painting all over again, putting a high-gloss spit-shine on my pedestals. I let him rub my legs, give the hairs underneath a good stroking, the hairs getting shorter as he moved higher. He raised his head off the alley floor and up to the level of his exploring hands, sniffing at my crotch like a crazed horndog. I jerked, the guy's perfect snout hitting home.

I was packing heat in my pants, my cock swelling up faster than the LA River in a rainstorm. The bozo had a real good nose for the Grade-A. He nuzzled my meat, bringing his meathooks round to hook onto my cheeks.

I grasped his blond hair. It was soft as chick's down, same colour. I yanked his gourd back, grated, 'You want a taste of my beefsteak, you wait 'til I give it to you.'

He liked that rough stuff. His eyes lit up like a movie premiere.

I shoved him backwards. He squatted down on his haunches on the dirty alley floor. I slanted my zipper southward, down over the airship-shaped bulge in my pants, nice and slow. Taylor licked thick red lips with his pretty pink tongue.

I whipped my rod out, the mounting pressure making the both of us sweat. I was blazing full-bore, the sudden onset of twisted sex getting a big rise out of me. I gripped my dong at the base and smacked Taylor's face with the hood and shaft.

He rocked back on his heels, rocked forward. His eyes were glazed. He was drooling like Rin-Tin-Tin. I clocked his perfect profile with another dick-slap.

I really fanned his mug with meat, the brisk whapping sounds filling the hot air, making both our faces flush. Precome bubbled my slit. It was strange, stimulating. I grabbed up my balls into a hairy knot and shoved sac and all down into matinee idol Taylor's mouth.

The cowboy chomped down on my nuts. I whacked his nose with my carrot. He eased up on the baubles, started sucking. The guy nursed my sac with sweet, sensitive tugging that brought more tears of joy to my slit.

It'd been a long time between lovin' for me, a parched, rocky patch of trail. The gorgeous hunk of man at my feet, the sensual pull of his plush mouthflaps on my pouch, the tease of his tongue on my testes, sent me rocketing to the rim and beyond.

'I'm coming!' I yodelled.

'All over me!' he implored.

I jerked back and blasted, letting him have it in the face, in his hair, all over the front of his Rodeo Drive shirt, each pump of my fist blasting forth a new load of steaming hot sperm. To coat and soothe the savage submissive.

His case was simple. Otto Von Deutsch, his domineering director of a 101 oaters and more had gone missing, and big Mack Taylor wanted him back. Apparently, the manly movie star needed to be ridden hard at work, as well as in private life. He needed Von Deutsch's dictatorial directorial hand to guide him, and no one could tell him where the studio hack had strayed.

Gower Gulch was where I moseyed on over. Every two-bit studio churning out the horse operas to the adoring herds was located on this strip of Hollywood real estate. If there were Western questions to chase, here's where I'd saddle the answers.

Only, I found myself roping air, not missing directors. None of the extras loafing around the dusty lots knew anything, the slattern gossip at the local chow palace chewing on empty. Even my contact at Rancho Pictures, Von Deutsch's studio, couldn't give me a lead. He worked the flak department, we'd worked on a couple of X-rated scenes in his apartment together. But he just didn't know. One day Otto Von Deutsch was stomping a studio soundstage in his leather knee-highs, bullwhipping a posse of hams with his leather tongue, and the next day he was gone.

It didn't make sense. No one seemed to be scouting the rugged tinsel terrain for the missing moviemaker. Except one lonely cowpoke who craved the lash of his whip. Von Deutsch was a holy terror, with fewer friends than a leprous loan shark. But still, someone at the studio should've been mounting a search party.

And that someone should've been C B Trojan, head honcho of Rancho Pictures. I cornered the lunk in his office, late one night, using an unlatched window as my means of introduction.

'Where's Von Deutsch?' I gargled, rousing the man from a script.

He looked up, startled. 'How–how did you get in? Who are you?'

'Werner Strauss, German secret police,' I cracked back in my best male Marlene Dietrich. 'I'm working with US Immigration. Otto Von Deutsch is in the country illegally. He's got a wife and five hungry glockenspiels back home in Hamburg.'

Trojan rose out of his leather perch, a tall bird, with a peregrine beak and grey eagle eyes, nest of white hair. 'Otto Von Deutsch isn't even German. He was born in Bismarck, North Dakota.'

The guy strode up to me and gripped my elbow, pirouetted my form doorward. 'Now, get out of here before I call the real police.'

He was used to getting his way in his own private fiefdom, didn't like it when I shrugged off his talons, sent him flapping back to his roost with a stiff arm.

I advanced on the ginzo, ditching the German accent, bringing out my muscle act. 'You're going to tell me where –'

'Please, don't hit me!' he grovelled, hinging at the knees, dusting the shag with his caps. 'I'll do anything you say!'

I stopped short, standing tall over the man. Where had I seen this act before? Yup, he was staring at my crotch, and I was filling it.

For an older bird, he wasn't bad-looking, knew a thing or two about handling men, from years of experience. He coveted my cock like it was the Oscar he'd never get, rubbing his hands up and down my swelling length.

My pants draped around my ankles, like the studio hotshot. He pumped me skin-on-foreskin with one hand, fondled my hanging balls with the other. As I made with the potty mouth, to properly put him in his erotic place. Like, 'You worthless sack of crud.' Or 'You snivelling worm.' He liked the words tough, more than the actions, the cock just as hard as Taylor had.

'Suck my dick, you Hollywoodland phony,' I hissed.

He didn't have mike-fright. He inhaled my bloated purple knob and the pink swollen pipe backing it up. My own knees buckled. He bobbed his head back and forth, sucking quick and tight and wet, and deep.

Saliva drooled out of the corners of his sealed mouth, all along my dripping shaft. I gave him all I had, and more, pressing my balls up against his chin, my prong buried in his gob, slanted down his drain. I fucked his kisser and lungs, plunging back and forth with a bucking intensity.

I jerked back just in time. 'Eat my ass, you heinous hunk of horse droppings!'

His eyes glittered like the twisted dreams of a million

Tinseltown hopefuls. He eagerly kneed around to my backside. I grabbed onto his silver mane, held him still.

'Now, where's Otto Von Deutsch?'

He looked at my smooth mounded bottom, my glaring eyes. He wetted his lips, swallowed his Adam's apple. I shuddered my rump, rippling the taut skin on my puffy posterior. Winning him over.

'He–he changed his name, his face, his mannerisms. He's Howard Glitz now, director of, hopefully, screwball comedies and song-and-dance movies – for the big studios.'

'Huh?'

'Yes, yes! He was suffering a severe case of typecasting, always forced to do Westerns, for B-studios and below. So, he devised this extreme make-over to break free of the ... reins, so to speak.'

It was just crazy enough to work, in La La Land.

'How did he get you to swear to secrecy, pile of piles?'

Trojan shrugged. 'He promised me ten per cent of the gross on his first ten non-Western pictures, with an option for 20 more.'

It sounded like a kosher deal.

I cut the man loose, to roam his trembling hands all over my ass. He caressed one rounded cheek, the other, both.

I stuck my backside in his face, barked, 'Eat it!'

His tongue went in so fast I thought I'd been cattle-prodded. He squirmed his wet sticker wildly all around my manhole, splitting my cheeks wide with his hands. Then he lapped like a steer at a salt lick, lathering my crack, stroking the smooth, sensitive skin of my ass cleavage over and over with his tongue.

'Fuck my butt! Stick your tongue inside my asshole!'

He jumped to obey, rocketing his pink blade into my rump opening. He sunk inside my anus right down to the lips, his and mine. Then he pulled back, pushed forward, chuffing my chute with his budded wet organ of delight.

I gripped my dick and fisted. My balls exploded, shaft

jumping in my hand, semen blazing a trail out of the tip of my cock. I stained the big wig's desk and clotted his carpet. He'd have it no other way.

'So, spill. What's the story? Where's Otto Von Deutsch?'

That was Mack Taylor again, making with the macho trail boss lingo again. We were camped out in the ranch-sized living room of his Hollywood Hills hacienda. I looked around at the opulence that a collection of make-believe Westerns could buy, and I liked what I ogled.

'Getting tough again, Mack?'

He stood, all six-four of him in a stretched plaid shirt and Levis, neckerchief and pair of heeled cowboy boots. He cut a mighty impressive figure, the kind I could get used to. 'You holding out on me, dick?'

I squashed the cigarette I'd been sucking on, rose laconically up on my hindquarters. Then I drew both pointed forefingers, lightning fast, thumped them into Mack's chest. He tumbled backwards, over a footstool and onto his stool.

'Get on all-fours,' I gravelled. 'And skin off those skintights.'

He looked up at me, his lamps now gussied with lust. He flipped over, hit the floor animal-style, popped his pants button and slid the denim over his butt and down to his knees.

His cheeks were tanned like the desert, smooth, rounded dunes. My cock swelled at the sight. I unholstered my rod, squatted in behind the butt, slapped cheek with my dick.

'Yes!' Mack bleated. 'Fuck my ass! Please, fuck my ass!'

'I'm calling the shots here, pardner,' I retorted, putting him in his place. Then putting my dick in its place – in between his hot taut buttocks.

He moaned, and I grunted, frotted. I pumped his crack, smacked his cheeks around, spurring the fleshy hills on to shivering, the man to whimpering. My cock pulsed pure hot pleasure, riding up and down the smooth, sensitive skin of his butt cleavage. My balls boiled.

I pulled back, out. 'Got any gun oil?'

This pack horse had it all. He fumbled a tube of slickener out of a pocket of his jeans and handed it back to me, sneaking a quick peek at my quirt.

I whacked his ass for his impudence. Then greased my iron, his petulant pucker. When we were well and truly slippery, I plugged his wanton need, shoving my shining cap up against his starfish.

He bucked. I pulled back, struck again, and again, poking at his pucker 'til he was groaning with want. Then I hit hard, busting his ring and ramming his chute.

'Yes!' he cried, my dick sinking into his anus like a plough into moistened earth.

His man-sleeve was tight, hot, like the rest of his body. My cock throbbed inside him. He squeezed it even tighter with his ass walls.

I gripped his hips and slammed back and forth in his chute, fucking his butt, riding roughshod. He clawed up his own hanging erection and tugged on it like it was the bridle of a runaway bronc. My thighs cracked off his buns, like pistol shots, my cock churning his anus like some homesteaders churn butter.

I reared back and let out a 'Yaaahoooooo!' waving my right arm around. Bringing my right hand crashing down on the man's ass, ecstasy bursting out of my balls and rocketing up my butt-buried shaft, spraying against Mack's bowels.

He jerked jism out of his own dick, shuddering, bucking, mewling.

'You don't need Von Deutsch,' I informed him afterwards, as he milked the last drops of seed out of my sprouter with his mouth. 'You've got me now. Any objections?'

He looked up from between my legs, attached to my shooter, down on his knees. He wagged his head from side to side, the answer he knew I was looking for.

With the dough I'd lassoed out of the head honcho of Rancho Pictures, and with cowboy Mack Taylor on permanent retainer, I'd just carved out a nice little spread for myself.

Some guys are tough; some guys have toughness thrust upon them.

Counting to Ten
by Elizabeth Cage

ONE

He makes me count each time his hand contacts the naked flesh of my exposed arse. The first slap is always a shock, the sting a fusion of pleasure and pain in equal measure.

I remember the first time he asserted his authority. We had been out for a meal at an out-of-town restaurant. On the way back, he drove into a public car park and put his red Mercedes in a space at the far end. It was a summer evening, and still half light. I wondered why we had stopped, but before I could ask he ordered me to strip off in the car. I smiled. It seemed like a sexy idea, so I slipped out of my short silky dress and lacy boy-shorts and leant back in the passenger seat, the leather upholstery sweaty against my naked skin. I have small, neat breasts so I don't often wear a bra. Feeling pleased with myself for meeting the dare and getting a frisson of excitement every time someone walked across the car park, I waited for him to kiss me. Instead he told me calmly that he wanted me to get out of the car and walk to the other side of the car park.

I was taken aback. Surely he was joking? But the expression on his face, the intensity of his grey-blue eyes said otherwise. He repeated his request, waiting for my response. My hand was gripping the door handle, undecided. What if someone saw me? Maybe that was the point. Shaking, I swung my legs round, my heels scrunching on the gravel. The first few steps were tentative, but there was no one else around at that moment and the warm breeze tickled my skin and I felt strangely liberated. I made it to the other side. I looked over to the car for approval. I needed his approval. He gave me a tight smile and I wondered if I had passed the test. Walking back was much harder.

Afterwards, when he dropped me home, I found myself hugely turned on and I was sure we would make love. But he informed me quietly that he was going away on business for a week and I was forbidden to pleasure myself until he came back. I was stunned. Another test.

When he returned, he brought me a gift. He told me he had made it especially for me. But first he needed to know if I had obeyed his instruction. I had. When his lips brushed against my neck before moving down my body, inch by inch, I thought I would explode with desire and lust. I came with such force as soon as he entered me, my whole being racked with violent spasms. He waited until I was satiated with pleasure, overwhelmed with inexplicable feelings of tenderness for him. Then he placed my hand on the gift that he brought for me, an elegant whip that he had crafted himself from long strands of soft but strong black leather. He took it from me, and began to trail it along the length of my pale skin, from my chin down my exposed belly and breasts, to my thighs, knees, ankles, and the tips of my crimson-painted toes. It felt sensual, the leather strands caressing, like an attentive lover. He let the leather tails dangle over my mouth, brushing my lips. Then he told me to kiss the whip. And I did.

TWO

We had been dating for two weeks when I realised that I was already lost.

I had arrived at his house to be greeted by a note pinned on the door. "Strip before you knock." I had spent hours getting ready, and was wearing a stunning brand new boned corset dress with a flowing crushed velvet skirt slit to the thigh to show off my long slim legs. But even so, I removed all my clothing, dismantling my carefully constructed outfit. Standing on the doorstep in my spiky black heels I felt suddenly self conscious. His house was partly shielded from the road and passers-by with trees. Even so, there was always the possibility that someone might call by, might discover me naked. It was thrilling but scary at the same time. But it was the knowledge that I was doing it for him that turned me on. He made me wait for what felt like ages, vulnerable and exposed, and I could feel and smell my own increasing wetness. The scent of my lust was intoxicating. Finally, the door opened and I almost melted when he told me to go upstairs and lie down on the bed. Unquestioningly, I obeyed. The bed, which was draped with a black rubber sheet, had steel handcuffs attached to each corner in readiness. I picked up the velvet-lined blindfold on the bedside table and put it on, making sure it was fastened properly. Lying there, engulfed in darkness, every fibre of my being was awake and alert to the slightest sound, the slightest movement. I heard footsteps on the stairs and my body tensed. I waited for him to speak, longing to hear his voice, but I had to endure the silence while he attached the cuffs to my slim wrists and ankles, so I was wide open. He ran a fingernail down between my breasts, lightly scraping the surface of my milk-white skin. I groaned, floating as I lost myself in the sensation of his hands exploring my eager body. He trailed a finger in my mouth, and I began to lick the tip, letting my head roll back onto the pillow. Then without warning he pulled his fingers away and rammed them hard inside my shaved cunt. It hurt. I jerked my hips and yelped. He responded by forcing a huge ball-gag into my mouth and securing it tightly. I thought I would choke as I struggled to breathe. He ignored my muffled cries and proceeded to probe me roughly, pinching and squeezing my nipples without mercy. But my cunt was dripping.

THREE

I had only known him for three weeks when he made me beg. He had left me chained to a hook in the ceiling, my arms aching, my arse patterned with familiar red marks from the spanking he had administered a few hours earlier. It seemed like an eternity before he returned, and I had started to lose track of time, my arms numb. He told me dispassionately that the marks were already fading, and I knew what to expect. Tears stung my eyes as he brought his hand down hard on my already tender flesh.

I yelped. He ordered me to beg.

'Please,' I whimpered.

'Please what?'

'Please, master. More.'

FOUR

As he raises his hand to bring down the fourth blow, I say out loud, 'Four.' My mouth is dry. I remember how he celebrated our anniversary, our first four weeks together. We were in the woods. He took me from behind. Then he tied me to a big oak tree and whipped me till my arse and thighs were black and blue.

FIVE

I am on my hands and knees because in this position the skin is stretched taut so I can feel the full force of each blow. He has rained five blows, after each stroke running his fingers over my engorged pussy lips to see how wet I am. It always amuses him.

SIX

We are at midpoint now. He pauses for a moment. He needs to prepare himself for the final six strokes. I can rest briefly and get my breath back.

Last time we were in the Jacuzzi together at the private club we go to, he told me to touch another man, to run my fingers along the length of this total stranger's stiff cock. Later, he ordered me to masturbate this man in front of the others in the steam room. At least six men were watching me, playing with themselves, as jets of come shot into my hair, over my breasts, in my face.

SEVEN
The pain is overwhelming now. I lose my will. I give it to him. His choices are mine. I am his instrument. I am a slave to obsessive love and my own desires and needs. I live for his words, his instructions. He is my life. My life is his.

EIGHT
He exercises impeccable self-control and judgement but I am not sure I can take much more. It is a familiar feeling. Involuntarily I draw a sharp intake of breath as I hear the resounding slap when his hand meets my arse with measured force. Instinctively I want to wriggle to protect my throbbing buttocks but I know this is not allowed.

NINE
The penultimate blow. I know he will make this one especially severe.

At 9 p.m. last night he looped a length of rope around my wrists, tying them in front, and led me over to the banisters. Lifting my arms high above my head, until I was almost on tiptoe, he pulled the rope and fastened it tightly to the rail at the top. Next, he clipped a chain onto my collar and wound it around the upright part of the banister, making it almost impossible for me to turn my head. He then went into the kitchen and returned holding a cut-throat razor. He pressed it to my face. My stomach flipped and I heard my voice, barely recognisable, asking him to stop. But he ignored my pleas and ordered me firmly to keep very still. I tried not to tremble as I felt the blade against my skin as he deftly cut through the straps of my creamy silk camisole. It fell to the

71

ground. Then he turned his attention to my silky boy-shorts. I thought I would pass out with fear, my eyes wide as he pressed the blade against me, slicing through the fabric like a knife in butter.

He put the razor down and picked up the whip, ordering me to open my legs wider, but my body felt limp, so he forced them apart, letting one finger dip into the honeyed crevice between my thighs. He moved the whip between my legs, caressing, teasing, carefully pressing the hard metal top against me. It slid in easily, too easily. He laughed and informed me that I clearly love the whip. I protested weakly but there is no doubt that my cunt loves this whip. My cunt doesn't lie. Then, as my muscles began to grip the source of my pleasure and pain, he slowly removed it and brought it down hard on me, three times in quick succession. He stopped for a moment and knelt down to kiss my throbbing flesh. Then he straightened up and lovingly pushed the hair away from my face, stroking my eyebrows with his fingertips, while his hard cock pressed into my back. I wanted him so desperately. Finally he took pity and released me. Exhausted, I almost sank down but his hands were around me, supporting my weight. Scooping me into his arms he carried me into the bedroom, setting me down beside the ornate full-length mirror beside the dressing table. He told me to look at the lovely patterns on my arse, tracing his fingers gently along the outlines of the red marks that striped my skin. 'From me to you. With love.'

Then he lifted me onto the bed and very slowly and gently, and with more tenderness than anyone had ever shown before, he made love to me. As the first of many orgasms racked my body, the sensations were so powerful, so intense, I was almost unconscious from the beauty of it. 'I love the way you hurt me, master,' I sobbed. 'I want you to mark me. Permanently.'

But he already had.

TEN

The final blow. I brace myself as he raises his hand much higher to get a better angle, so he can bring it down with all the force he can muster. It is hard to breathe. He administers one last resounding stroke. My arms and legs buckle and I collapse onto the floor.

He slips a finger inside me and I come.

It ends. Until the next time ...

No Reservations
by Alana James

'I am sorry to announce that our electronic reservations system is down. I repeat, there will be no reservations on this journey.'

This was exactly why I shouldn't be forced to travel standard class, among all these loud, sweaty, *normal* people. Bloody new company policy. Damn recession. Passengers began throwing themselves into empty seats on the last train of the night from London to Bristol, sending their little brats to scout ahead. It really wasn't my fault if I pushed a few out of my way.

I slowed down, ignoring the disgusting throng around me, and assessed the situation. I have a preference system when it comes to sitting next to someone on public transport: young women, female students, teenage girls, older women. To be avoided at all costs: young children, teenage boys, other businessmen and especially old people. There was a young filly a few seats up, on her own, not exactly beautiful but not bad either. I fixed my most charming smile in place, but a spotty teenage boy snuck into *my* seat. The greasy kid had the audacity to smirk at me too.

I continued along the carriage, *accidentally* whacking the boy on the head with my briefcase. No, no, urgh, definitely not, OK. There was a woman sitting hunched against the window: middle-aged, plain and just the sort to spend the journey quietly completing crosswords. She'd do.

The prince charming smile flashed back on, 'Excuse me, may I sit here please?'

'What?' she muttered, 'Oh yes, of course.'

Now *I* smirked at the poor sods still trying to sit down. I broke out my laptop and began calmly working away. I felt confidently superior, typing and emailing, liaising with the outside world while the commoners read their magazines and listened to their music.

It surprised me when the little lady sat next to me took out her own laptop a couple of hours into the journey. She hardly looked the type to understand what one did, never mind own one. I couldn't help grinning at the tiny pink machine; my own silver, widescreen, 3G processing machine glinted smugly. I ignored her and carried on working with a sense of self-importance. Until the battery ran out five minutes later. The *only* plug socket was being used by the pink novelty next door. I snuck a peek at the power monitor on the woman's screen; ten per cent charged. Damn it, I could hardly ask to use the socket now. Bloody standard class.

I shut my laptop, brimming with frustration. Fuck all to do now. At first I drummed my fingers then I shut my eyes for a while. I wasn't accustomed to unproductiveness. I opened my eyes again and glanced around for something to do. I certainly wasn't going to go and get my own standard-class coffee.

I wondered what was keeping the lady next to me so busy. Emailing the grandkids? Playing online bingo? Leaning right back in my seat I looked over at the screen. She wasn't on the net, but typing into a word document. Curious. She had glasses on but was still squinting at the screen oblivious to my attentions. What was she typing?

Reginald quivered at the feet of his mistress. She towered above him magnificently in her shiny black stiletto boots. Quickly he obeyed her order and began licking those boots eagerly. Reginald made murmuring, appreciative noises and

76

gasped with pleasure when Mistress raised one foot, allowing him to press his tongue to the dirty sole.

What on earth was this? Crazy old bat. Imagine sitting on a train typing *that*. Still, I wondered what would happen next...

Suddenly Mistress used her foot to flick Reginald away by the chin. It hurt like it always did but increased his arousal as it also always did. 'Get up and bend yourself over the bed,' she commanded. Reginald did as asked, the cold sheets cool on his naked skin.

God, this was filthy. My cock stirred in my trousers, confusingly.

His mistress took her time approaching the bed. Reginald wondered which instrument of torture she would choose tonight. Without warning the air swooshed and a hard paddle cracked onto Reginald's backside. Merciless smacks of the paddle rained down on his flesh, turning his cheeks flaming red. Reginald cried out in pain and ecstasy, his shaft swollen and rubbing against the sheets.

My own dick was swelling too. I moved my laptop onto my lap, to cover the bulge. I certainly never let a woman dominate me, yet it was having the same effect as the girl-on-girl porn I watched. I felt compelled to keep reading.

In between strokes of the paddle Mistress started to stroke her slave's cock from behind, and slide her fingers up between his cheeks ...

'Curiosity killed the cat, you know.'

I jumped at the sound of the woman's voice.

'What's your name, boy?' the woman sat next to me asked. I turned to give her an odious look; no one addressed me as "boy". My face fell when I saw the look on her face. I couldn't figure out how but her soft middle-aged features, the fleshy jowls of her neck, had hardened into a stern expression.

'I said, what's your name – boy,' she repeated loudly.

'Paul,' I stammered despite myself.

'Paul.' She pronounced my name like she was reprimanding a small child. 'I know you've been watching over my shoulder. You're being a naughty boy, aren't you?'

I felt myself flush uncharacteristically, feeling ashamed and lost for words. I'd been caught like a dirty voyeur. 'I, I ... I'm sorry.'

'I'm sorry – Ma'am,' the little lady corrected, fixing her beady rimmed eyes on mine.

'Sorry, Ma'am,' I muttered quietly. I looked around the carriage hoping no one was hearing this. At the same time, this exchange was oddly thrilling. My cock was still hard under the laptop, the images from her typing were buzzing around my head.

There was a silence between us. I shifted uncomfortably in my seat as she looked me up and down, assessing me. I felt smaller than I ever had in my life, my shoulders hunched as my body folded in on itself. This feeling of minuteness was out of my realm of experience. I supposed it was how I normally made other people feel.

'Take that laptop off your lap, boy,' Ma'am commanded sharply. Her tone brooked no disobedience. I did as instructed, packing the machine into my case, hyper-aware of the raging hard-on this act exposed. I thought about crossing my legs to hide it, but something told me that was a bad idea.

'Now you're going to make it up to me,' she continued, licking her lips. Ma'am looked in her element; her features were hard but I could see a flush of excitement on her cheeks. She was really quite stunning. 'You're going to stand up, walk to the end of the aisle and go into the bathroom. You will close the door but not lock it.'

That said she turned away from me and began closing down her laptop. I couldn't believe this. What a nerve she had. So I'd peeked over her shoulder – big deal.

But what I really couldn't understand was that I was considering obeying her. My shaft had swelled with a rush of blood; it seemed to be pulling me in the direction Ma'am had indicated. A battle ensued between the man I had been before this journey, and my newly submissive cock. In the end it was an odd sense of propriety that gave me the reason to submit. I could hardly sit there with my bulging dick on display.

Like a horny automaton I rose from my seat and began walking along the aisle, cock-first. The little lady remained seated, face impassive. I waited in the toilet cubicle, shifting from one foot to another. It was one of the designs to accommodate passengers with wheelchairs; it was flat along one wall but bulged out in a semi-circle on the other side. Plenty of room then, but for what? The wait seemed to last for ever. I listened to my heartbeat thump-thumping and eventually identified this new sensation as nervousness. Just when I decided I couldn't bear the squirming any more, Ma'am arrived and locked the door behind her.

She looked taller, imposing. Her back was poker straight, her face steely. I found myself admiring her presence; her persona had shifted upwards while mine seemed to be sliding down. I backed away from her without thinking, up against the far wall.

'Now, look here. Let's not pretend this is going ...' I began but was cut off.

'Did you like what you saw, boy?'

'What?' Her question threw me off.

'On my computer screen. You see, I'm an erotic writer and that is my latest novel. It's all about male submission,' Ma'am paused, allowing this to sink in. 'To make sure I get the techniques right I have to practise in my free time. You're going to help me.'

'I'm not sure about that, ahem,' I spluttered, coughing. There was a charged moment where we each stared at the other. I noticed the way her dark brown hair framed her face, the glint in her eyes and the deep red pucker of her lips. She stared me down, looking magnificent. Then, with my face burning, I nodded in acquiescence.

'Turn around and face the mirror.' She gave me time to obey. 'Good boy. I'm not going to make you lick my shoes but I am going to punish you for being a dirty voyeur.'

'You were the one writing that stuff in a public place,' I objected without thinking, 'hardly my fault for seeing it.'

Smack! Her hand hit my ass. Smack! She hit the other cheek. I couldn't believe this lady was spanking me. On a train. In standard class. As she continued the blows I felt my ass warming and my cock growing even stiffer. Each blow shook my body, delivering a sharp pain that somehow transformed itself into a tingling pleasure. I gripped the handrail below my waist and found my legs shifting, spreading apart.

'You're enjoying it, aren't you?' I didn't know what to say, it was too embarrassing. 'Answer me, boy.'

'Yes, yes,' I admitted through clenched teeth. She brought her hand down on my cheeks again. This was becoming quite painful. And overwhelmingly pleasurable. Every nerve-ending in my ass was on fire, yet yearning for more.

'Yes, what?'

'Yes, Ma'am!' I realised this was what was expected. I felt like Reginald, unable to resist the demands of his mistress.

'Drop your trousers. I want to see your ass glowing,' she instructed. Her voice was as cold as steel.

I looked at myself in the mirror. I looked bewildered; confusion and indecision flickered across my face. Beads of sweat had gathered at my brow, my mouth was pursed and I was pure white. I felt my body tremble as my hands slowly released the handrail, and undid the buckle on my belt. I was shaking so much it took a long time to undo it, and then unzip myself. Each second that passed seemed to make it more real that I was doing this.

Eventually I lowered my trousers, briefly hoping they

wouldn't get too creased then hoping *I* wouldn't crumple too much. Ma'am stepped closer, so that I could see her in the mirror and feel her breath in my ear. She bit into my earlobe. I gasped at the sudden sharp pain, at the sweetness of feeling her touch my bare skin. She tugged at the bottom of my briefs. I got the hint. Turning bright red, I slowly forced myself to pull my shorts down to my shaky knees.

Ma'am drew back and I could sense her eyes on my arse. This was ridiculous, standing in a train toilet exposing myself to a complete stranger. What if she decided she was displeased and walked out, letting anyone in the corridor see me like this? I shut my eyes, unwilling to see myself so clearly. I had to admit, the fear of being exposed was only making me more aroused.

I heard a rustle behind me. Her handbag. I realised she had brought her handbag with her. Surely she didn't carry a paddle around? The tension I felt as I waited for her next move was unbearable. My chest heaved as I struggled to maintain control. My dick shuddered with excitement and fear.

Then it came – a stinging lash across my whole ass. Not a paddle. More like a whip. Ma'am lashed again and again, criss-crossing the strokes painfully on my already sore cheeks. I forced my eyes open, ignoring my reflection and staring behind me. I saw the glorious little woman stretch her arm back, preparing to whip me again. It was the looped power cable for her laptop. Such a mundane object inflicting so much pain. And humiliating pleasure.

'Your ass is getting nice and red,' she informed me mockingly between lashes. 'I bet your cock is getting harder too.'

'Yes, Ma'am,' I spat out, not wanting to bring any more punishment down on myself. Truth was, the brunt of each strike was forcing me forwards and rubbing my shaft against the slick handrail. I was overcome with conflicting emotions; fear, embarrassment, loathing and respect for this

81

woman. She had grown in my eyes. She was strong and self assured, indomitable.

'Let's try something else, shall we?' she said teasingly. My body seized with anticipation but my cock remained hard as I rubbed it over the rail. I watched in the bathroom mirror as she fiddled with the power cable. Ma'am was twisting it in her hand until only the rectangular power box was free, hanging on a small length of cable. I gulped. She spanked.

The box was harder than her hand, weightier than the cord. Each smack heated my arse up even more, until it was burning all over. The box itself was still hot from being recently used and I started to really sweat from the heat I felt. The heavy load of each strike shoved me against the handrail stronger than ever. I panted as the friction worked my dick over.

I cried out too loudly when I felt Ma'am's fingers slip into the cleft of my ass between spanks, teasing the tight hole there. I'd let a couple of girls do that before, but they'd never done it like this. Her fingers ran all the way up and down the cleft, stopping every so often to snake into my arsehole. Even as I continued to rub my cock against the handrail, I found myself pushing my butt out, silently begging her to fuck me with her fingers.

'Tell me what you want, boy', Ma'am whispered into my ear, licking the spot she had bitten before. I groaned, unable to respond at first, unable to think with her hand still teasing me.

'Fill me, please,' I pleaded. I felt a finger slide just inside my hole.

'Please what?' she whispered in response, a slight laugh in her voice.

'Please, Ma'am.'

Finally, she thrust her finger all the way in, filling me deeper than any woman before her. Ma'am worked her finger back and forth, fucking me hard. I heard her drop the power cable from her other hand and then she ran her free hand over the sore points on my ass. All at once she pushed her finger in as far as it could go, bit me hard on the back of the neck and pinched one of the welts on my rear.

The shock of the pain combined with the pleasure, the strange emotions she had produced in me and the tightness in my balls, to tip me over the edge. My jizz spurted out, dripping over the rail and I swear I screamed with the release.

As the last of the come spat out, Ma'am withdrew her finger and rubbed my cheeks soothingly. I could learn to love a woman like this, I thought.

She made me clean my spunk up, as was only proper I supposed, while she washed her hands in the tiny automatic sink and packed the power cable away. I pulled my trousers and briefs up, but I still didn't feel composed. My hair was sweaty and there were large damp patches on my shirt under my arms. I shook myself, trying to regain some sense of who I was.

Ma'am calmly opened the toilet door and stalked back to her seat. I cringed at the man standing outside, hoping he hadn't been there long enough to hear too much. When I got back to the seat I saw that this strong beautiful woman had, after all, taken out a puzzle book. I didn't do anything, just sat there with my arse sore, shell-shocked, trying to make some sense out of what had just happened.

We didn't speak again until the train was nearing the end of the line. I found I couldn't just leave it there. There had to be *more*.

'Excuse me,' I croaked. 'I was, erm, wondering if you, ahem, had a business card. So I can look up your novels.'

Ma'am looked at me and smiled, truly the smile of a predator that has caught its prey. To my disbelief, my dick lurched once more.

'Why yes, of course. You feel free to look up my novels anytime.' She took a smart-looking card out of her purse and handed it over, her hand briefly clasping mine firmly.

When we were arriving into Bristol a tinny announcement came over the tannoy, 'Thank you for travelling with us. Once again I am sorry that there were no reservations on this journey.'

The Best Laid Plans
by Alex Jordaine

Jacqui was running out of time. Right from the start there had been a strong spark of mutual attraction between the oversexed young brunette and Anne, the woman she was temporarily lodging with while her rooms in the university hall of residence were being renovated. Jacqui had firmly resolved to fully ignite that spark before leaving Anne's home. However she was due to move back to the hall of residence the next morning and had already packed most of the few belongings she had with her at Anne's place. So it was now or never.

It was easy to understand why Jacqui was so attracted to Anne, an agelessly beautiful woman with short ash-blonde hair, high cheekbones and a wide, sensuous mouth. Anne's eyes were perhaps her most striking feature. They were pale blue like a tropical lagoon; you could fall into her eyes they were so blue. She had a well-shaped figure as well: soft and full, slim but rounded. Jacqui could tell Anne was lonely, though. She had a husband she clearly adored but he made his living as a musician and was constantly on the road.

Jacqui seriously had the hots for Anne who had an air of control about her that really turned the young woman on. She had spent every night since moving into Anne's home pleasuring herself in bed while fantasising about having sex with her. Jacqui had found herself increasingly yearning for the real thing though and had finally determined to make that happen before she moved out. But she was cutting it very fine. It had to be today or it wasn't going to happen at all.

Jacqui's first manoeuvre on that now-or-never day was to go into her bedroom in the mid-afternoon, strip naked and lie on top of the bed masturbating energetically, having first "accidentally" left her bedroom door half open. When Anne walked by her bedroom as Jacqui had known she eventually would, she couldn't help but look her way. Seeing that Jacqui was stark naked and masturbating vigorously, her fingers working like fury between the lips of her sex, Anne averted her gaze straight away and quietly shut the door.

It was enough, Jacqui was sure of it. As she continued masturbating hard, her pussy now dripping with wetness, she kept replaying that moment. She could see again Anne's blue eyes flashing over her and widening with excitement as she took in what she was doing to herself so eagerly with her busy fingers. In that short moment Anne had registered unmistakable sexual desire before regaining her composure, averting her gaze and silently shutting Jacqui's bedroom door.

The thought of what she'd just orchestrated was incredibly arousing to Jacqui, causing a surge of desire to run through her like electricity. She plunged her fingers into her dripping pussy again and brought herself to a powerful orgasm, gasping and moaning, all the time thinking of the look of desire she'd seen on Anne's face.

Jacqui then showered, brushed her hair, applied a little make-up and slipped her silk robe on over her naked form. It was time to take things to the next stage, which she knew she needed to do quickly. She had to strike while the iron was hot. Jacqui adjusted her shimmering robe to ensure it was loose at the top, leaving the swell of her breasts enticingly exposed, and pressed on with her mission to seduce the lovely Anne.

Jacqui padded bare footed downstairs and into the living

room. The windows were curtained in dark patterned linen and heavy net. There were several throw rugs on the parquet floor, black-lacquered furniture, a black leather suite.

Anne was seated on the couch, leafing through a glossy magazine. She looked up and gave Jacqui a pleasant smile that gave nothing away. There was not even a glint in the eye to say that she had been affected by what she'd seen her doing, nothing to acknowledge the desire that Jacqui was now sure she felt for her.

'Anything I can do for you?' Jacqui asked meaningfully, raising a sculptured eyebrow. Her body was tingling with anticipation.

'You could get dressed,' Anne suggested, barely looking up from her magazine. It was not an encouraging response.

Jacqui however was undeterred. She was determined, come what may, to have sex with Anne before the day was out. 'I'll go and put some clothes on,' she said.

'Fine,' Anne replied, flicking onto the next page of the magazine. She appeared to be indifference personified but she couldn't fool Jacqui. She had seen that look in Anne's eyes when she'd been outside her bedroom earlier.

When Jacqui returned to the living room she was still bare footed but was otherwise dressed ... sort of. She had on a red singlet that was very tight, her beautiful breasts pressed against the thin cotton, her erect nipples plainly visible. She was also wearing an extremely tight pair of soft black leather shorts. They were cut very high indeed, exposing smooth bare thighs, the cleft of her sex and much of the curves of her shapely backside.

Jacqui felt very aroused by the shameless way she was exposing her body to Anne. 'I must have put on weight recently,' she said giving her a wicked grin. 'I could barely squeeze into these leather shorts.'

Jacqui certainly had put on weight lately but only in the sense that she'd regained all the pounds she'd lost a few months ago when she'd dieted for a while with unduly excessive zeal. She'd bought the tight leather shorts when her weight had been at its lowest. They'd looked incredibly sexy and provocative then. They looked more than that now: they looked positively obscene.

Anne put her magazine onto the coffee table. 'I can well imagine you had difficulty squeezing into your shorts,' she said, hardly taking her eyes off her this time. 'I'm surprised you can even move in them.'

'Oh, I can do that all right,' Jacqui said, giving Anne a sexy, full-face smile, a *challenging* smile. She did a seductive little walk, sashaying back and forth in front of Anne, her unbound breasts swaying and jiggling and her thighs quivering and rubbing together as she moved.

Nothing could disguise the desire she saw in Anne's eyes as she flaunted herself in front of her. Jacqui was wearing no underwear and the thin strip of black leather was pulled up tight between her pussy lips, rubbing against the wetness of her sex. It aroused her even more, making her nipples poke even more insistently against the scanty red cotton top.

'I think you've made your point – or should I say points.' Anne smiled, eyeing her rigidly erect nipples as they strained against the tight material of her singlet. Rising gracefully to her feet, she stood in front of Jacqui. She then reached out for her, took her by the waist and pulled her close. The two women looked at each other for a long moment and then Anne put her warm lips to Jacqui's and kissed her hard. The women kissed deeply, Anne exploring Jacqui's mouth with her wet tongue, letting her breathe her hot breath. 'This is what you want, isn't it,' she whispered.

'Yes,' Jacqui replied urgently. 'And a lot more besides.'

'You want to go all the way?'

'I'd *love* to go all the way.'

'Even though you know that I'm a happily married woman?'

'That just makes you all the more appealing to me,' Jacqui said, 'all the more tempting.'

'And that makes you a bad girl, doesn't it?' Anne's impossibly blue eyes were shining brightly.

'That makes me a bad girl,' Jacqui agreed.

'Let's sit together on the couch and take things from there,' Anne suggested huskily.

'Yes, let's,' Jacqui replied, her own voice hoarse with excitement, and they sat down side by side. Things were really going Jacqui's way, she thought. She felt in control of the situation.

Then all of a sudden she didn't. 'As far as I'm concerned bad girls like you need to be punished,' Anne said, her voice suddenly cold. She took Jacqui firmly by the hands and pulled her across her lap. Jacqui turned and looked over her shoulder at Anne, catching the gleam of determination in her eye. Jacqui may not have been in control any more but she as sure as hell knew what was coming next and it made her shiver with excitement, made her heart race wildly in her chest. She was about to get rather more than she'd planned for today – and that was just fine by her.

Jacqui cried out when the first stinging blow came down, the flat of Anne's hand slapping firmly down on her rear cheeks. It was an explosion of pain, a raw livid sensation that turned her skin red. Then the second stroke came down and it was as sharp as the first, the sound reverberating around the room. Anne held Jacqui down, keeping her in place across her lap. She spanked her three more times in quick succession. The pain escalated with each blow, a fire building on her flesh.

But those few blows were only the beginning. Anne continued unremittingly, cracking her hand down onto Jacqui's backside with relentless vigour, following one smack after another in swift succession. The cheeks of her rear smarted with a heat that made her tense and squirm and, with each slap, her tensing and squirming increased.

The robust spanking went on and on, the living room continuing to echo with the sound of hand on naked flesh.

Anne simply did not let up and the pain burnt hotly on Jacqui's backside, sinking ever deeper. But with the pain came pleasure and throughout the beating Jacqui could feel its heat build up in her sex, which rubbed excitingly against the thin strip of leather pressing tightly against it.

Jacqui wanted, no, *craved* more. She arched her back, lifting herself, offering the reddened cheeks of her arse to Anne's fiery strokes. The pain was intense. So was the pleasure. When the smacks landed now it was almost as if her pussy had been caressed. She was slick with her juices. She was soaking, dribbles of love juice smearing her thighs. Her clitoris throbbed with pleasure as she lifted herself, opening her thighs so that Anne's fingers landed on the soaked leather between the lips of her pussy, landed too on the lips themselves.

At last the thrashing stopped and Jacqui twisted round to see the curves of her cruelly spanked backside. They were dark red against the black of the ultra-brief leather shorts, the imprint of Anne's fingers on her flesh merging into a deep flush of pain. Jacqui tried to get up but Anne kept her in place. She began to run her hand over the soreness of Jacqui's rear, feeling the burning heat that she had inflicted on her skin. Jacqui sighed as Anne went on to stroke her fingers between her wet thighs. She pushed the leather deeper between her pussy lips, making her shudder with desire.

Jacqui sighed again and shuddered even more as Anne's fingers pressed harder against the wet material. She arched her back, on the verge of orgasm as Anne pressed her fingers harder still against the love juice-soaked leather. Then Anne stopped, pushing Jacqui off her lap. 'Bend over the edge of the couch and wait,' she ordered, getting to her feet.

Jacqui was soon in position, breathing heavily with sexual arousal. The blood was pounding in her veins and her throat was dry. She closed her eyes, wondering excitedly what form of chastisement Anne was going to subject her to next. She also wondered, as she listened to her leaving the room, how long she'd make her wait for it.

Anne was not gone long. Jacqui's eyes flew open and she cried out loudly as the crop came down in a swift trajectory, striking a line of fire across her backside. 'I gave up riding years ago,' Anne said. 'But I hung on to this. I always knew it would come in handy one day.' Jacqui let out another loud cry of pain as Anne brought the crop down again, further inflaming her backside as it bit into her flesh. Then she sliced the crop through the air a third time and a further red-hot strike landed across Jacqui's rear cheeks. It was followed by another harsh stroke, and then another.

Anne began to beat Jacqui with even greater ferocity, slicing more and more red heat through her body. The crop struck her bum in a regular harsh rhythm, and each time it cracked against her skin it planted a flame-hot line on her flesh. Jacqui responded to each sharp strike with a cry of pain ... and pleasure. A red heat seemed to be burning into her skin, sinking deeper and deeper.

Anne started to strike more quickly, inflicting even more excruciating pain on her, which brought with it even more intoxicating pleasure too, and Jacqui's cries came faster and faster. Tremors of pleasure-pain ran through her body and she could feel the heat blazing on the cheeks of her backside, the skin raised and imprinted with the pattern of the crop.

Jacqui lost count of the number of times Anne used the riding crop on her, but when the beating was finally over and she was allowed to stand up, her flesh was quivering and burning with both great pain and great pleasure.

Jacqui suddenly felt conscious of the passage of time. The light outside the window had faded and the colours in the room had dimmed and were tinged with shadows. It was evident that afternoon had morphed into evening during the course of her prolonged punishment.

And that punishment had left her feeling incredibly randy, horny beyond belief, the heat of desire sweeping through her body. Her clit was buzzing, burning. She was ripe, ready. Now for what she'd actually planned for, Jacqui smiled to herself salaciously. Now for some pure – correction, *im*pure sex with Anne.

But Anne had other ideas altogether. 'That's all you're getting out of me,' she said with grim finality, her voice cold. Her beautiful face had hardened into a mask. 'I want you to go to your bedroom now, shut the door, strip off your little fuck-me outfit and spend the rest of your time under this roof lying on the bed and playing with yourself – like you were doing this afternoon for my benefit.' She went on: 'I want you to leave my home at the crack of dawn and never return. You might have been determined to seduce me today, Jacqui, but I was even more determined that you wouldn't. I told you I'm a happily married woman. I'm also monogamous, and that's the way I'm going to stay.'

Jacqui did as she'd been told, climaxing time and again as she masturbated deliriously for hours on end, her skin marked deeply by the heavy chastisement Anne had inflicted on her. As her fingers pressed into her sex over and over, penetrating hard and fast, she luxuriated in her own sticky wetness, the heat of her pussy, the pulse of her clit. The sensations were exquisite, racking her body with spasms of erotic delight.

The pain Jacqui was still suffering as a result of her earlier beatings – the bruises and lacerations from which she knew would take days to fade – and the knowledge of what had caused that pain in the first place made her epic masturbation session and the multiple orgasms that went with it a hundred times more intense. She climaxed repeatedly, wanting the waves of ecstasy to go on and on until she could do no more. Her sex was soaking, drenched from her frantic self ministrations. The bedspread was wet with juice.

Jacqui's night of onanistic excess did finally come to an end, though. It *had* to come to an end because Anne had been very specific in her instructions. There was nothing else for it, nothing that could be done; it was over. Jacqui left Anne's home when dawn's early light had dimmed all but the brightest stars, closing the front door behind her as quietly as Anne had closed her bedroom door the day before.

Coated
by Kay Jaybee

The sound of his own breathing rattled in his ears. He tried to calm himself, to moisten his dehydrated throat and cracked lips. He was afraid, and yet surprised by his fear.

It wasn't as if this had been sprung on him. This was a fantasy that he'd lived with for years; a desire that had consumed him to the point of obsession ever since, as a teenager, he'd seen it in a porn movie.

Ever since he'd glimpsed her out the corner of his eye, standing aloof and alone, looking out of the window of the bus – a creature totally displaced by her surroundings – he'd known she was the one to help him fulfil his dreams. He also knew he had to do something. Get this fixation out of his system – whatever it took.

He'd taken the same bus the next day, and the next. She'd been there, same time, same place, every day. On the fourth day, he spoke to her.

Peering down her imperial nose, a small crinkle forming across her forehead, the woman sneered at him with utter disdain. She didn't actually say, '*How dare you presume to talk to me?*' But her thoughts were crystal clear.

That was six weeks ago. Six slow weeks of gradual understanding via little actual conversation. The woman, whose name he still didn't know, had understood what he needed, without him having to tell her; it was just the fine details that he needed to explain and embellish.

He shivered against the chill draft that crept through the gaps between the metal doors that separated the warehouse, in which he stood, from the outside world. The drone of the traffic as it rumbled by the building was both a comfort and a distraction. It was good to know that an ordinary world lay beyond the bare brick walls and empty echoing space, but he feared discovery.

She'd directed him to this disused warehouse. 'Somewhere suitable', she'd called it, and then left him. He wasn't sure exactly how long ago it had been since he'd been wordlessly stripped and tied. Her face had revealed nothing. No pleasure at the sight of his nakedness, at his stiff cock, at his willingness to obey her bitten off requests.

The jeans and white shirt he'd selected to wear with such care had been discarded without a second thought. He could see them now, dusty on the hard cold concrete floor.

Shifting his bare feet, he flexed his toes, trying to warm them a little, wishing he was miles away, but knowing he had to be there. It wasn't the collar and chain around his neck, fastening him as if he was a wild animal that kept him in place. It was the prospect of the fantasy fulfilment to come.

His shoulder muscles had begun to cramp. Attempting to gain some relief he hunched them up and down as best he could, but was hampered as his arms had been tethered via another long chain to one of the metal props that supported the roof.

The creak of the door as it opened was so subtle that, if he hadn't been listening intently for it, he would have missed it altogether.

Footsteps, soft and yet with deliberate pace, approached him from behind. He could turn, but he didn't. If it wasn't her, then he didn't want to see who it was; but he was sure it was her, for even in those few steps he could feel her self-assured air.

He wondered, as the atmosphere tensed around them,

what she was wearing. Not high-heeled boots if the quietness of her footfall was anything to go by. His thoughts were interrupted by the abrupt tug on the chain that held his wrists. It was yanked hard, and he found his arms raised above his head. The drag on the metal was not released until he was balanced on the balls of his feet, hanging like a cur, every muscle in his arms and back straining as the scrape of steel on iron told him his unseen companion was wrapping the slack around the girder.

Sahara dryness claimed his mouth and throat as he waited, hardly daring to breathe. A finger was playing over his backside, and with every touch of the soft pad of her digit, and the accompanying scratch of a fingernail, his flesh puckered into a spread of goosebumps.

A pale elegant hand reached around him, picked up the lead that hung from his neck, and twisted it so it ran directly down his spine. The occasional dig at his neck told him that his attendant was knotting it, attaching an object to the end. Once she'd finished, something heavy and cylindrical pulled his neck back a little as it hung, swinging against the backs of his legs. He didn't want to think about what it might be. Beyond his initial request to have his erotic requirements met, this evening was hers to do with as she liked. That had been the deal.

She stood before him then.

He'd had an image of how she might appear. He'd been wrong; and he was glad. This was much better than where his clichéd imagination had taken him. There was no black or scarlet, no PVC, and no shiny leather. Her hair, rather than being tied back in a severe ponytail, was flowing free around her apricot shoulders, its chestnut sheen positively glowing as it framed her face and narrowed green eyes. A figure-hugging satin cat-suit in darkest burgundy, the trousers of which accentuated her long legs and slim waist, while the neckline plunged at her chest, showing him that her cleavage was everything he'd hoped it would be.

Even with her bare shoeless feet, the effect was more erotic and tempting than if she'd been dressed as a dominatrix on heat. His dick swung alarmingly towards her, and he felt embarrassed at his uncompromising need to have her.

Assessing him with shrewd eyes, the woman traced her fingers over his lips, down his neck and towards his nipples. Squeezing his eyes shut, he anxiously felt his orgasm rising far too soon. Desperate to calm down, frantic not to spunk merely from the application of this amazing creature's fingertips, he exhaled slowly and gently. The joints in his arms began to scream in his ears; and the more he thought about reaching his hands out to fondle her breasts through the silky material, the more his inability to move haunted him.

Stepping forward, she leant towards his right nipple, clasping her mouth around it. The moan that hissed through his teeth morphed into a yelp as she bit into his skin, nipping and snapping at his mini-teat until it pinked and poked against her exploring tongue.

He was so engrossed in feeling the burning pleasure she was creating across his chest that he didn't notice her fish a brilliantly polished set of silver clamps from her trouser pocket.

As the tools sharp zigzag teeth buried themselves into his unsuspecting nipple, the dominatrix swapped to his left side, her attention both deflecting him from, and adding to, his pain. The knowledge that the second clamp was coming only increased his tension, making the hurt far worse than when he'd been taken by surprise.

Once he was adorned to her liking, his mistress stood back and critically examined his new appearance. Nodding to herself with satisfaction, she retreated behind him.

The chain allowed him to twist, but with the first step he took in an attempt to see what she was doing, a fresh wave of delicious suffering coursed through every nerve in his body. The movement jarred his body and radiated a strangled heat towards his shoulders. Thinking better of turning again, he waited impatiently for her next move. Balancing on one foot at a time, flexing each in turn to ease the strain in his legs, he forced himself to wait without begging her to hurry up. His desire for her to speed up collided with his desire to make this experience last.

A silence descended on the room and, for a split second, he panicked. Surely she wouldn't have gone again, not before her part of the bargain had been fulfilled? *Why can't I hear her moving about?*

His alarm was short lived, for the soft rustle of a plastic bag reassured him of her presence. Then, with deliberate precision, she stood in front of him, and paraded the items she'd removed from the bag in a short line on the dirty floor.

The butterflies that had been churning in his stomach accelerated. She had bought it all. Exactly as he'd requested. He swallowed very carefully. *Do I really want this?* The shudder of his cock answered his own question as his gaze flickered from the equipment to the woman who'd bought it. The hint of a nipple poking from beneath her suit, and the mild increase in the heaving of her breasts gave her away. She was also excited, but in a much more controlled way.

She picked up the item at the end of the row. The wide black bristled brush flicked gratifyingly through her fingers. He was almost hypnotised by her handling of the decorator's tool, as if he could already feel the touch against his flesh, though it had yet to make contact.

He'd expected her to smooth it over and around his flushed and abused torso, but instead she gestured with her hands, ordering him to swivel around.

It was difficult to obey. The extra twist to the chain that tethered him shortened it a fraction as he moved, resulting in his feet rising higher, and all his weight shifting to his tiptoes.

Despite the cold of the room, sweat dotted his back as

well as his forehead. She waited just long enough for him to become impatient, but not long enough for him to plead, although the thought had entered his head. Then, just as the discomfort of his position was becoming all engrossing, he was distracted by the swipe of the bristles over his backside. Both soft and yet harsh at the same time, the brush was pressed against his skin with enough pressure for it to feel somewhere between bliss and anguish. There was no question – this woman was an expert.

With each sweep of the bristles his cock leapt, and he needed to concentrate harder than ever on not coming before she'd done what he most wanted.

Heady sensation swam behind his eyes. All those times he'd got off by coating small areas of himself in patches of emulsion. Watching it dull and harden against his skin, feeling each hair prickle and crack as the brush coated him, and his erection swelled. This was different though. Better. Much better.

Circling the brush in small rotations over his buttocks, he longed to implore her to move it higher, lower – anywhere else – for the remainder of his body was beginning to feel severely neglected. As she worked, the weighted lead at his neck kept being knocked, and as the mistress continued her obsession with his butt, working very carefully and precisely over his anus, he realised what the tool she'd attached was. The thought alone made him shudder afresh. He wasn't sure if he wanted to be right or not.

Kicking at his ankles, his tormentor widened his legs as far as possible within the confines of his restraints. Then, kneeling, she poked at the entrance to his butt with her warm agile tongue. Standing statue still, the discomfort he felt melted away as his whole being focused on what was happening to his arse. The pressure of the lead went slack. She'd picked up the end, and was playing with what he was convinced was a buttplug, at the winking opening of his hole.

Even before she pushed the plug into him, his stomach began to contract. Breathing deeply, doing his best to relax his clenched arse, he groaned out loud as the freshly lubed tool was eased into his vulnerable passage. His groan changed into a guttural yell, half of protest, half of pleasure at this new and unexpected experience.

Once the plug was fully inserted, the lead at his collar tightened, and his neck was craned back further, linked via the leather strap to his butt.

Now surely she'll do what I want – what I need!

As if hearing his silent pleas, his new mistress came back in front of him, her complexion flushed.

His eyes shot down her cleavage as she bent to the pot on the floor, and picked up the screwdriver, so neatly placed next to it.

The combination of his stomach churning in reaction to the presence of the buttplug, the strain in his arms, legs and neck, the pinch at his chest, and the extra surge of lust as she placed the screwdriver under the lid, and levered it off the paint tin, took him beyond confused to semi-delirious. This really was going to happen.

As he watched, the initial dipping of the brush seemed to happen in slow motion. Thick creamy white emulsion hung to the brush. She hovered the brush over the tin, knocking off the excess for a second, loose globules hitting the glossy substance and rippling across the surface.

Pausing, as if she was an artist trying to decide where to start on a challenging canvas, she roamed her eyes over every section of his body. Then, coming to a split-second decision, she drew the brush in one firm stripe across his torso.

Closing his eyes, he was instantly lost in sensation. The paint, cold and cloying, filled his navel and highlighted every muscle. Drying almost the second it hit his warm flesh, the emulsion tightened and plastered his skin, making him aware of every minute hair on his body.

Stroke after stroke she continued, every new set of brush marks coating his upper body, his back, and his legs. It was an unusual kind of discomfort. A discomfort he'd been desperate to experience ever since he'd seen body painting on that porn film over a decade ago. Over the years, this craving had reached almost obsessive proportions, dominating every sexual hope, every daily wank.

She took extra care around his nipples, the cool liquid counteracting with the burn of the clamps, as fresh waves of pain were caused when the brush knocked against the silver grips.

His breathing quickened. There was still bare skin that longed to feel the stroke of the brush, and the trail of oozing paint that it left in its wake. He couldn't hold back though. It was too much. Everything felt too good.

'I'm gonna come!' His cry in the silence felt strange as it ricocheted around the warehouse walls.

She snapped her attention to his face, one look at him telling her he was serious.

It took less than four seconds for her to get where she wanted to be. The top half of the cat-suit was unzipped, and her luscious breasts fell free. Crouching directly in front of his cock, she wrapped one palm around his length, while continuing to apply gloppy liquid with the other hand to his left leg.

She shrieked as his white cream blasted her tits, covering her as effectively as the paint coated him. No words escaped her, but the mistress's eyes spoke volumes of satisfaction as the spunk dribbled down her naked breasts.

As the last of the come smeared her, she stood, and with a deft movement, freed his arms and removed the collar, although the buttplug was firmly left in place, the lead dangling, as if he'd suddenly grown a tail.

His shoulders cracked as he lowered his arms, and he took a second to rotate his neck – but only a second, for his companion was pointing to the paint-splattered floor.

He barely noticed the pain in his knees as he hurried to hit the concrete, keen to fulfil his part of the bargain. With every move of his body, the dried emulsion broke and splintered, piling new sensations on top of old, as he licked his own juices off the skin he'd dreamt about touching for over six weeks. As his tongue hit her nipples, she grabbed the clamps that were still adhered to his. Twisting them, she made him howl into her breasts with a gorgeous rush of smarting torture.

It was all she needed. A final dose of enjoying the agony she'd steadily inflicted on him. Leaning in closer, reaching round to pull the dildo from his rear, she started to spasm against his lapping tongue, the abrupt loss of the plug making him whine further.

He kept working, licking her tits faster, marvelling at the climax that rocked her, despite there being no contact with her cunt at all. She'd got off on pain. His pain.

Disguising his paint-peeling skin beneath his clothes, he didn't say anything as they made themselves presentable for the outside world. They hadn't talked all evening, and speech now didn't seem necessary. Something was nagging at him though. A realisation he hadn't expected: once wasn't enough.

She was the one who broke the silence, and as if reading his mind, said, 'You want to do this again, but you want it to hurt more. You want me to decorate your arse and then beat it.'

It wasn't a question. It was a fact. This was going to happen again.

And the truth was, he couldn't wait.

Personal Trainer
by K D Grace

The only people named Hawk are either on the pages of sleazy romance novels or in testosterone-crazed shoot-'em-up films. Hawk Sturgis looks like he could fit the bill in either case. His blond hair is a military buzz cut. His trousers are army surplus camouflage tucked into boots that look like they weigh several kilos each. The Rambo look is pulled together with a khaki muscle shirt that, for all I know, could be painted across hard pecs and washboard abs. I look him up and down thinking he's good looking in a strange GI Joe sort of way. And he looks me up and down like a drill sergeant with a new recruit, one he's not particularly pleased with.

Because he has insisted we meet at five in the morning, and it's still dark outside, I'm already mentally asking myself if I really want to do this. Then he barks. 'Davis, Penelope.'

In spite of myself, I snap to attention. My friend, Alison, warned me Hawk's methods are unorthodox. I think about Alison, all sleek and slender and glowing in her miniscule new swimsuit, and I grit my teeth. Getting up in the middle of the night may take some getting used to, but if it'll get me looking hot in my new bikini for the summer hols, I can live with it. And if Alison's fab new body is any indication of what the man can do, well, I can learn to salute. 'Call me Penny, please.'

He studies me from under tightly drawn brows. 'Barnet tells me you want to hire my services.'

'Barnet? Oh, Alison. Right. I do, yes. Come in. Tea? Coffee? Water?'

'No. Nothing. Barnet says you want the standard beach job. 'Zat right?'

'The standard beach job?'

He stops in the centre of the lounge and folds pile driver arms across his chest, giving me a tight-faced look that lets me know in no uncertain terms my ignorance is insufferable. 'Beach? Bathing costume?' His enormous hands drop to his hips, and he takes a step closer. 'You don't want to look like a lard-arse in your new bikini. 'Zat it?'

I blush hard. 'That about sums it up, yes.'

He gives me another disapproving onceover, like he can see every extra inch of pale, unfit flesh hiding beneath my baggy gym suit. 'Gonna cost you a hundred quid an hour,' he says.

I grab for the arm of the sofa like I've been gut punched. 'A hundred quid an hour?'

He nods.

'That's a little out of my price range.'

'You get what you pay for,' he says.

'I understand that, of course, I do.' I offer an anaemic smile. 'It's just, well, Alison said you were affordable. That's all.'

He holds me in his cold blue stare. 'Barnet was on the contingency plan. That's a different matter altogether, more demanding.'

I'm up at five in the fucking morning. How much more demanding can it be, I wonder. 'But it's more affordable?' I ask.

He shrugs. 'There are certain terms and conditions. Certain arrangements to be taken into account.'

'Tell me,' I say, feeling my heart hammering in my throat. I do not want to go to the beach this summer hiding behind a wrap or a sloppy T-shirt.

'Here are the terms.' He moves a step closer. 'You do exactly as I say at all times, and if you don't, you take the consequences without complaint. You do that, and I guarantee results by the end of our contract period.'

'OK,' I nod. 'And if I do exactly what you say to the end of our contract period, *then* what does it cost?'

He looks at me like I'm an imbecile. 'That is the cost.'

'That's all? That's it. I just have to do as you say?'

'Exactly as I say. At all times.'

'So, what's the catch?'

He folds his arms across his chest again and glares down at me. 'Look, do you want the contingency plan or not? If not, stop wasting my time. I got paying clients.' He turns toward the door.

'All right! All right. If you can get me the results you got for Alis ... for Barnet then I'll take the contingency plan.'

I'm expecting a handshake or a 'You won't regret it,' or something. Instead, he holds me in a cast-iron gaze until I start to squirm, folding my arms across my breasts, feeling like maybe he has X-ray vision. At last he speaks. 'You sure you're up for this level of commitment?'

'Yes, of course I am. I mean if Barnet can do it, surely I can do it, Mr Sturgis, Hawk.'

He grinds his teeth and his jaw clenches like a vice grip. 'You will address me as "sir" for the duration of our association, Davis. Are we clear?'

I square my shoulders even more square. 'Yes, sir, we're clear.'

'You will do exactly as I say.'

'Sir, yes, sir.'

'You will not question my authority. Ever. You got that?'

'Sir, yes, sir.'

He moves nose to nose with me, practically breathing fire. 'This is no joke, Davis. Man's body is his temple. Keeping it fit and healthy is serious business.'

'Yes, sir.' I figure now might not be the best time to tell him I'm not a man. Surely he must have noticed that – me with the tits and long hair and lippy and all.

'Good. Then we start now. I got a gym I use not far from here. This early we have it to ourselves, but only for an hour, so move your arse.' He nods towards the door.

I grab my car keys from the hook by the sink, but he shakes his head.

'We walk?'

He shakes his head again. 'We run.' Then he gives my trainer-clad body a sceptical look. 'I need to know how bad it is.'

When we finally arrive at the gym, and he unlocks the door, I'm thinking death is imminent. He places a meaty hand against my neck and eyeballs his chronograph to check my pulse. I'm wondering if it's even possible to count that fast. I'm not sure if the resulting grunt means it's acceptable, or that he's totally disgusted with my lack of fitness, but at least he's not dialling an ambulance.

He marches me at a fast trot to a back room with mirrored walls and free weights.

I head straight for the nearest weight bench. It's the perfect place to collapse and have a whimper. But I don't get far.

'Davis! About face!' he huffs.

And I'm standing at attention again, while he walks around me, hands on his hips muttering. 'Uh huh, mmm hmm, right.' He nods to my blue trainer bottoms. 'Take 'em off.'

'Sir?' My voice cracks.

'You want a beach job, I need to know what I've got to work with.'

'I have a leotard, back home. Believe me, it doesn't hide anything. If we could just wait–'

'Take. Them. Off.' Between each word he makes a stabbing motion at my trackie bottoms with an index finger that looks like it might be a registered weapon.

I shove the trousers down and step out of them, embarrassed by the comfy, and now sweaty, granny panties I wore to work out in. I never expected to have to display them.

'And the top.'

'Really, I'd feel a lot more comfortable if we could do this after I get home and then I'll just slip into the leotard and–'

'Davis, you will do as I say or find yourself another personal trainer. I will not tolerate insubordination.'

The thought of one hundred quid an hour flashes through my mind, followed in quick succession by the thought of a svelte, sleek new me in a red bikini, and I peel off the shirt to reveal an equally ugly white sports bra.

But he doesn't notice the bra or the knickers, instead he yells in my ear. 'Drop and give me ten!'

'Wha–'

'Make it 20. Now!'

I fall to the floor with all the grace of a wildebeest on ice, then I struggle through eight push-ups, arms trembling like I've got some spastic muscle disease just before I collapse on the floor in a heap.

And suddenly he's arched over me like he's gonna put some kind of painful wrestling move on me. But just as I muster the breath to beg for my life, he wraps one tree-trunk of an arm half around my waist and supports himself with the other. 'I'll spot you,' he says. 'When I say 20 push-ups, I mean 20 push-ups.' And there he is doing push-ups on top of my push-ups, all supported on three limbs, like a tripod, his hand splayed low on my belly, pulling me up every time he pumps up. He gives me just enough help to struggle through.

It's impossible for me to count. It's impossible for me to think of anything other than Hawk Sturgis arched over me, his big hand pressing dangerously close to my pubic bone, his camouflaged crotch raking against my granny-pantied arse with each upward thrust. When I'm finished, he hauls me to my feet, pressed tightly against acres of hard muscle, and I'm very aware that one of those hard muscles just happens to be his cock.

I'm surprised when he says, 'Not bad, Davis. Most women have no upper body conditioning. You'd think they'd work a little harder on those pecs, do a few more push-ups, some flies. After all, it's upper body conditioning that makes for good cleavage.' I don't know how he does it, but with a little shrug, and some sleight of hand, he unhooks my bra, slides the straps down off my shoulders and shoves it forward onto the floor. I try to cover myself with folded arms as he steps back and turns me to face him. 'You got nice full breasts, Davis.' He wedges my arms apart with his big hands and rakes a calloused thumb over each of my burgeoning nipples in doing so. 'A few push-ups, maybe some dumbbell flies and your cleavage will give every bloke on the beach wood.'

His gaze is like a magnet pulling my nipples all taut, and I wonder if it's my cleavage that has given him wood, or if it's just a permanent condition for the macho commando type. He motions for me to turn around, completely oblivious to the blush clawing its way up my chest and neck. 'Your glutes are nice and poochy, the kind that will look good in a thong. It is a thong, isn't it? Your bikini?'

Before I can utter an embarrassed no, he hooks a thick finger in the elastic of my knickers and tugs them down until my arse is on candid camera. He ignores my yelp of surprise and keeps a good grip on the elastic while he offers a running commentary on the foibles and glories of my bottom. 'No cellulite. That's good. Nice heart shape.' He cups each buttock and gives it a kneading squeeze. 'Needs some firming. Nothing a few squats, some hack squats and a good running regimen won't cure.'

He kneels so his nose is just inches away from my

exposed bottom, shoves the panties down until they pool around my ankles, then cups my arse cheeks like they're two melons he's contemplating at the market. And all the while he's contemplating my arse cheeks, his hot breath is blowing its way right up the valley in between, straight to my cunt, and my labia are parting like the Red Sea in full anticipation. Bloody hell! This isn't what I expected.

'Spread your legs, Davis,' he says. 'I need to get a feel of your thigh muscles.'

I do as he says, knowing full well that while he's feeling my thighs, he's getting a bird's eye view of my puss. Did Alison go through this? Did she mind? 'Cause each time I feel his breath on my slit, I mind less and less. As he squeezes and kneads my upper thigh muscles, the tip of his heavy thumb just grazes my swelling pout, and I jump and gasp at the delicious shock of it. It's like someone pressed the turned-on switch, and if I wasn't hot and bothered before, I certainly am now. I'm tilting my hips forward, gripping and relaxing, gripping and relaxing, giving all those girlie muscles a stealthy workout. I'm trying not to hump air in my efforts to reel in his hot breath and wrap it all around my grasping cunt.

'You're carrying a lot of tension below deck, Davis. You have regular sex?' he asks.

I respond with several fish gasps before I find my voice. 'Not regular, no.' I figure that'll be good news to him. That means I won't have to give up sex to stay focused while he rebuilds my body into a temple.

'Sex is like callisthenics on steroids,' he says. 'Damned important part of any training regimen. Any good one at least.'

Before I can utter my surprise, he says, 'We'll start out with three times a week. See how you manage that, then we'll work our way up from there.'

He ignores my sputters of shock and continues talking to my arse. 'Some people get really turned on by working out.

111

They need sex afterwards to unwind and relax. Others want sex before they work out. They like the extra rush of endorphins. Me,' he heaves a sigh that I feel on my pussy like a gale-force wind. 'Me, I could go either way. Sometimes both. Your body will tell you what works.'

I offer up a couple more fish gasps through a flaming blush before I manage to croak. 'You mean you want me to ... mmm ... to masturbate as a part of my training schedule?'

'I didn't say masturbate, did I, Davis? I said you should have sex. The wanking, well it'll do if you don't have a proper work-out partner. Mind you, masturbation's a good way to burn a few extra calories, I'll grant you that, so yeah, I'd say have a wank whenever you feel the urge. But I'm not talking about self-pleasure here. I'm talking about real, genuine bumping and grinding. There's no better workout.' He manoeuvres himself to kneel in front of me, moving his hands up over my hips and abs, deep massaging the muscles like they're dough and he plans to make some serious bread.

'But, I don't have a proper work-out partner,' I say, trying not to grind my hips against his massaging hands.

He gives me that how-long-must-I-suffer-fools look and shakes his head. 'Your body, I can do something about, Davis. But it's up to you to exercise the muscle between your ears.' He taps a finger against my temple, emphasising each word. 'There's just you and me. I'm your trainer *and* your work-out partner. That's what you pay me for.'

The light bulb finally comes on in my head, and my stomach manages half a flip-flop before the hand that has been massaging my abdominal muscles so expertly suddenly slides down until it nestles against my pubes. His thumb rakes my clit, causing me to offer up an undignified grunt. He knows he's found the control switch, and, holy crap, does he know how to use it! The rough pad of his thumb circles and rakes, and circles and rakes my nib until it feels like a lead weight straining against his fingers.

He nods to the bench I've been coveting, never taking his

steel-blue gaze off my face. The hand not circling and raking moves to cup and squeeze my tits in turn. Then he scooches me back, and back, and back, almost like he's herding me with his thumb on my clit until I plop down on the bench.

He shakes his head. 'The bench is not for sitting, Davis. Squat in front of it, and rest your elbows on it. This is a workout, remember? That's right, now open your legs and lift until your weight's on your elbows.' All the while he continues to circle and rake my joy button, until I'm completely in his power, and I'll do whatever he says, because the only other person who has touched my clit for ages is me.

'Mm hm,' he says, slipping his long index finger between my cunt lips and stroking. 'Just as I suspected. You need some serious relief of a sexual nature, Davis, or we're never gonna accomplish anything.' He slides his finger up into my hole, and I swear I've had cocks in me that weren't that thick. I go all ragdoll and limp, like he's supporting me just on his finger, and I'm squeezing and gripping like nobody's business.

'Jesus, Davis! That's one hard-gripping fanny you got there, and slick.' He lets out a low whistle as he squeezes another sausage finger into my pout, and I'm wondering what the hell his cock's gonna be like with fingers that size.

'Put your feet on my shoulders,' he orders. He doesn't offer to help, and I figure that's a part of the workout, all designed to make me look good in my bikini. When my weight is supported on his shoulders and my elbows, he goes exploring. Face first.

Even his tongue is well-muscled. And long. It's almost like it's not a part of him, the way it wriggles and squirms and eats at me, all hungry and animal-like. He holds my labia splayed wide with his thumbs while his tongue darts in and out of my hole, then laps and slurps and presses at my clit. Then he starts all over again. He does this until I'm out-of-my-mind hot, and he has me squirming and writhing and babbling like some porn star. Then he starts nursing on my clit like he's a newborn who's just found a tit full of milk.

And I come. Jesus, how I come! I'm bucking and bouncing, banging my elbow on the edge of the bench and howling like some banshee on heat.

Then he pulls away, all wet and slick with my pussy juices, and I hear his fly unzip as he brings out the big gun.

I scrabble and squirm for a good view of his very military cock standing at full attention. It's as substantial and as pumped as he is. I feel a little twinge of fear at the size of him, but not for long, because my pussy's pouty and anxious, greedy enough to swallow him down whole, and he knows it. He teases my lips wide open with one hand. With the other, he manoeuvres into position, then he shoves and grunts his way in, pushing my knees up against my tits in his efforts. Sweet Jesus, I have never been so totally and completely full of cock! As he begins to hump, I wrap my legs around his waist and hold on.

He doesn't support my arse with his hands. He makes me support my own weight, pressing up to meet him every time he thrusts into me. And the harder I press, the better the rub against my marbled clit.

'Good girl,' he breathes, reaching up to cup and knead my tits. 'We get some of that pent-up energy of yours released and we'll have you in shape in no time.' He rakes my nipples to hard, raw points against his thumbs. Then he sucks me like he's trying to suck me inside out. I bounce and squirm and buck all over the weight bench, digging my heels into his kidneys, riding Hawk Sturgis like he's a bucking bronco and I'm a cowgirl.

I reckon he's a master of timing. He suddenly stops playing with my tits, grabs onto my hips like he'll crush bone and jackhammers my cunt. He's holding his breath, baring his teeth like an angry lion, and I'm hanging on for dear life, every muscle in my body trembling and twitching.

114

It's like some kind of feral battle cry when he comes, rattling the mirrors on the wall and raising the hair on the back of my neck. I can feel his cock go into convulsions in my hard grip, and that's enough to kick-start my own convulsions. And we come and come and come.

Even a hardened military man like Hawk Sturgis needs a little recovery time after all that coming. And when at last his pecs aren't heaving like bellows, he speaks. 'That's a good start, Davis.' He pulls away and tucks his cock back into the camouflage. Then while he's wiping my pussy with the work-out towel, he lays a splayed hand low on my belly. 'I reckon you'll be sore tomorrow after your first day. Nothing to worry about. I know a few massage techniques that'll work out the kinks.' He offers me a serious look. 'No pain, no gain.'

'Permission to speak freely, sir,' I say, watching him wipe and caress my pout.

'What is it, Davis?' He doesn't look up. He seems totally focused on his efforts.

'I know you said sex is a part of my training, but I'm wondering if–'

'Damn right sex is a part of your training,' he interrupts. 'A very important part. But,' he heaves a chest-expanding sigh. 'Man's gotta have some compensation, doesn't he? You don't work for free, do you?'

'No, sir.'

'You got a problem with that?'

'No, sir.'

'Good.' He offers me a smile that makes him look much less GI Joe, much more pussy-creaming hottie. 'Don't worry, Davis. You'll toughen up just fine. And come summer holidays, well I reckon you'll heat up the beach to boiling point in your new bikini. Tomorrow we'll do some squats and work your legs and glutes.'

'Same time?'

He nods. 'We'll start with a run from your flat. But if you're too sore, we might start with sex instead to loosen you up.'

Suddenly getting up at five doesn't seem so bad.

We hear a key turn in the lock, and the lights in the outer hall switch on. I'm scrambling back into my clothes and Hawk Sturgis is watching me like he's dreaming up his next torture session. But I don't care. If he makes me come this good after every workout, I'm more than willing to honour the terms and conditions of the contingency plan, and I may just return my more modest bikini for a thong after all.

As we step out of the gym into the anaemic daylight that has appeared while we were occupied inside, he slips an arm around me and nods in the direction of my flat. 'We won't run back this morning, since you're just getting started and all. I can tell by the way you move you're feeling a bit tender.' He slides a hand down my back to cup my arse and give it a gentle knead. 'In fact I think once we get back to your flat, I'll see if I can't loosen up some of those muscles for you so you won't be so sore tomorrow.'

In a peripheral glance, I can't help noticing the camouflage front of his trousers is struggling for containment. And I'm willing to bet the slight swagger in his step has nothing to do with the hard workout or the heavy boots. Come to think of it, I'm sure I haven't worked off my debt for the day yet, and that thought makes my pussy quiver right along with all the other muscles that are quivering and trembling from their first real workout in a long time. Suddenly, I'm very much looking forward to getting in good shape. After all, my body is my temple. It's serious business keeping it fit and healthy.

Support Your Local Store
by Alex Severn

Gareth had only moved here recently so he was still getting his bearings locally. Every Sunday morning he got up really early and walked to the local store at the top of his street. They sell pretty much everything; with a 24-hour WalMart on their doorstep they need to, but it's the Sunday paper that he really goes to buy.

His eyes always strayed to the tabloids with the screaming headlines about some soap star shagging some footballer and the cheaper ones always have some gorgeous woman wearing very little on the cover with a promise of something more revealing inside. The papers are nicely hidden from the view of whichever bored and sleepy-eyed assistant is unlucky enough to be working so he can have a flick through and turn himself on with the pictures for a good few seconds.

But this Sunday ... He practically leapt out of his skin at the sound of her voice.

'She might be OK but she's only a picture – wouldn't you prefer to see a real woman?'

He jerked his head around guiltily to see her.

She must have been in her 40s with soft long blonde hair that was in great condition, tanned and classy looking. She was very tall, almost Amazonian. Her light cream-coloured summer dress buttoned down the front matched the heat of the day that was building early. She smiled at him and revelled in his embarrassment, making him feel like a schoolboy caught reading a dirty mag by the teacher.

Before Gareth could speak she moved over closer to him; she was almost brushing against his body and stooped to pick up the *Sunday Boobs* or whatever the paper calls itself and picked out the page with a young blonde, topless, with the tiniest thong you've ever seen.

'Very cute, I suppose, but a bit young, don't you think? Don't you think my tits are better?'

With that, she unbuttoned her dress to her stomach and the most gorgeous, firm tanned brown tits spilt out, only inches from him.

Her nipples were a dark chocolate brown and, to Gareth, the perfect size. He held his breath, unable to move or speak. She laughed at him softly and said, 'Can't you cope with a woman in the flesh then or do you need a bit of encouragement?'

She took his hand gently and placed it on her left breast, pushing the back of his hand further onto her warm soft mound. The feel of her flesh broke the spell and, almost in a trance, he started to stroke, rub and fondle her nipple, thrilled to see it harden for him.

'Suck me now.'

It was a command, not a request, but he was only too happy to comply. He ducked his head down and licked, sucked and nibbled on her juicy left nipple while he brought his hand up to coax and play with the other. He was rewarded by her deep moans of raw pleasure.

With a quick, urgent movement she moved her hand downwards and he felt fingers straying down to his now hard cock, pushing down his shorts and freeing his shaft which was jutting skywards towards her.

As if waking from a dream he realised they were in the aisle of a shop and he tore his mouth away from her tits and jerked backwards, saying, 'We can't do this here, somebody will see us.'

She just smiled as if to reassure him. 'The assistant is reading way up there – she wouldn't even notice an orgy.'

And when he felt her fingers circle his length and start to rub him and massage his tight balls, he knew no power on earth could make him resist anyway.

His eyes focused on her stomach. Her last two buttons were still done up and he could see the outline of light-coloured hair under her dress which told him she hadn't bothered with any knickers. She saw how hungry his gaze was and, with an even deeper, even filthier smile, she unbuttoned completely and, as the dress fell to the floor, she stepped out of it.

He was mesmerised and transfixed by the view. Fabulous tits with bullet hard nipples pointed at him, a thick bush of blonde curls framing a pussy that he could see was already glistening wet and gaping open for him. She opened her long slender legs wide, leant back against the shelves and said, 'Fuck me now. I want you inside me.'

His head spinning, his heart beating ever faster, he drove his rock-hard length into her and felt as if he was sinking into an Aladdin's Cave of treasures, her soft soaking wet lips circled his shaft and, as he pushed deeper and deeper, she wrapped one leg around his waist to coax him further in. He'd never felt so big or hard but she wanted – needed – more and she arched her back away from him, changing the angle so that he felt her lips were in control of him totally. Then, they both came together, panting and gasping as they broke away from each other breathlessly.

Reality began to kick in as he realised he had just been screwing in the middle of a shop on the way to buy the morning paper when he heard another female voice say, 'I should be calling the police on you two, you know that, don't you?'

They both turned to see the young brunette assistant. She must have been much nearer the man's age than the woman's. Perhaps she hadn't been quite as engrossed in her reading as they'd thought.

But even as she half-threatened calling the police, she started to strip off her dark green overall and, very quickly, she was standing there, naked, with a freshly shaved pussy and small but very tempting tits on display for him.

Her face creased into a wide grin. 'If you don't want me to make that call, get down on your knees and lick my cunt dry. If you make it good enough, I can forget what you filthy pair have been up to.'

God knows why but he half turned towards the woman he had just been screwing – almost as if checking for her permission – but his hesitation brought a sharp response from the assistant.

'Look, I know where this tart lives; I've seen her drooling over young kids before in here. She won't be getting away so easily, I'm sure her husband would love to know how she has been spending her Sunday morning.'

The tall blonde froze.

He lightly dropped to his knees in front of the brunette. They all knew she was in charge now; what she wanted, she was going to get ...

She was already saturated by the time his tongue got there; he knew she must have been touching herself while they had been fucking, oblivious to the show they had been putting on. She felt hot and wet as he licked and explored the raised hard nub of her delicious clit and savoured the pink and purple folds of her labia. Out the corner of his eye he could see the blonde, still naked, rubbing her own lips, fingers plunging deeper and deeper into her gaping pleasure dome and that just drove him on to make sure the assistant got what she wanted. He lapped every crevice, every silk soft fold and, finally, he felt the waves of orgasm flowing through her body, her muscles spasm and she pushed his head away, breathing heavily.

The man looked around for his clothes assuming this was over, needing to get home and have a very cold shower

With a confidence of someone who knows they are pulling all the strings the assistant strolled over to the blonde and casually fondled her tits, drawing her mouth closer to hers. She was an inch away from kissing her full on the lips, but the older woman jerked her head way and in a quick but savage moment, lashed out with her hand and slapped the younger girl's face hard, saying, 'Keep away from me, you little bitch.'

The other's face darkened, her teeth almost clenched and, simultaneously, Gareth and the blonde realised she had made a pretty serious misjudgement.

'You're going to be very sorry for that, blondie. I was going to let you get dressed and go home to your loving husband, but now ... By the way, when I saw what was going to happen I switched the CCTV on you. We could all be stars in a nice little porno, couldn't we?'

She moved quickly to close the shop door, turning the sign round to tell any callers they were closed. God knows how she would explain that to her bosses if they received any complaints, but it didn't seem to worry her much.

'Go through to the storeroom quickly. It's in the back there.'

The other two shuffled along, still naked and vulnerable, both wanting to find the courage and the words to take her on but both failing.

The room was small and crowded with boxes and containers. As the girl closed the door, she switched on a dim light and shadows flickered across their bodies.

She was obviously thinking how to play this, but suddenly her mind seemed to be made up.

She delved into a box and came up with a length of cord, perhaps used for binding heavy boxes together, but as she flourished it triumphantly it was clear she had a very different use for it in mind.

She smiled slowly at the other woman, telling her, 'Right you, bend over, touch your toes ... if you can, darling.'

The blonde victim opened her mouth to speak but thought better of it, knowing she would be better to get this over with quickly.

His eyes were drawn to the way she was posed. He saw her peach-shaped bum, shivered at the swell of her lips showing between her cheeks and couldn't fail to see the moisture forming between them again ...

The director of this play handed the cord to him.

'Whip her. Let her know she's been bad, right? She needs to be taught a lesson and I want to watch you doing it.'

He didn't hesitate and, though he might try and tell himself he had no choice and he was only doing it because he had to, deep inside he was excited by the prospect, God he wanted to feel the power and the pleasure of knowing she would feel the pain.

He thrashed down on her back first, watching her wince, but the brunette hissed at him, 'On her arse, stupid. Let's make it so sore, she'll remember who the boss is for a long time.'

He changed the angle of the punishment, flaying her bum repeatedly. A couple of times the cord caught her crevice – he knew it must have beat against her labia – and he was almost breathless with excitement until the assistant motioned him to stop.

'That's enough now. Put the rope down.'

The blonde woman straightened up with an effort, her face flushed and sweating.

The assistant moved closer to both of them and casually reached her hand down to his cock, smiling at how hard it had become during the beating and grabbing it roughly. She began to rub him up and down roughly and, without stopping this movement, she reached across and hooked first one, then two fingers inside the other woman's open wet pussy.

As she coaxed juice from the gaping hole she started to lick her fingers, tasting the come. The man saw the blonde open her legs wider, silently pleading for more and this only heightened his own arousal as he felt fingers pulling, stroking and manipulating his hard shaft.

He came suddenly and helplessly.

Abruptly, it was over.

The play was at an end, it seemed, and the brunette told them both to get dressed and clear out of the shop, with a final reminder that she could always use the tape if she felt like it.

He left the shop first, wondering how he was going to tell his girlfriend why he was so late in getting the Sunday paper, but the blonde lingered a little until both the women could see he was out of earshot.

The shop assistant spoke first.

'That was good, yeah, but maybe I was too quick to catch you with him? Next time why don't I let you give him a blowjob? I know you like a nice hard cock in your mouth.'

The blonde smiled beautifully and put her arms around the other woman.

'I do – but what I really want is to feel that rope again. How about you teach me just how good it feels when a woman is doing the punishing. And I haven't licked you out myself for ages now ...'

Custom was really slow at the shop that morning.

Waiting in Vein
by Giselle Renarde

'Put the knife down, Julie.' Elsha took a step forward, extending an unwavering hand. 'Here, give it to me.'

Julie let her lips curl into a playful grin. 'No.' When she clutched the heavy butcher's knife between her naked breasts, the dull edge of the steel blade chilled her flesh.

'God, next you'll be asking me to strangle you.' Elsha shook her head. 'It's like you've got a death wish, chickadee.'

With a chuckle, Julie traced the knife slowly down her breast. 'A death wish? I'm not *that* fucked up.'

Elsha laughed. When she reached for the knife, Julie relinquished it to her steady grip. 'Where do you get these crazy ideas, child?'

Julie's cunt tremored in approval. She loved it when Elsha called her a child. Names helped her to feel more submissive. With a shrug, she fell back on the couch and propped her head against a throw pillow. 'I know people.'

'Scary people,' Elsha replied.

'Not scary, just intense.' Julie stared up at Elsha, at her braided hair and long skirt. The girl dressed like a pioneer. But maybe Elsha's uninterest in trumping the social order was precisely her appeal. Julie had known enough rebels. Elsha was safe. Too safe? Boring? Julie's body cried out for action. She wanted to be cut. It was something new. She had to try it. She had to try everything. Life was short. *Do it now*. Her veins coursed with adrenaline. 'Don't you ever just want to grab life by the horns and fuck the shit out of it?'

Elsha stood in the middle of the carpet, eyes wide and lingering. When Julie's gaze fell to the big knife in her hand, her toes curled and her cunt constricted. She could feel the juice gliding from her naked slit, down past her asshole, and coating the couch. Elsha would be upset by the mess, and that made Julie smile. A surge of annoyance ran through her body. The waiting killed her. Running her fingers through her short hair, she pulled on it until the upward pressure on her roots gave her a needed dose of pain. But self-imposed fury never was as good as the measured grief Elsha doled out.

Grasping chunks of her own hair between her fingers, Julie cried, 'Cut me! Just fucking cut me already, will you?'

When Elsha walked with complete calm to the kitchen and slid the knife into the butcher's block, Julie's muscles seized with rage. She'd relegated her sexual self to a life of submission, and it made her crazy. She made demands out of turn because she wanted experiences that defied the mundane life she'd always led. But, ultimately, it was Elsha's call, and that put her over the edge.

Writhing on the couch, she pulled harder on her hair. 'Please don't put that knife away! You have to cut me, please!'

As always, her wrath provoked no reaction but a smile on Elsha's lips. After a moment of maddening silence, Elsha began her slow return to the living room, one foot in front of the other. Clicking disapproving teeth, she shook her head as she stretched their clean cotton tea towels end to end. They were long and beige with a pattern of little white flowers around the edges. Julie's heart hammered at her ribcage when it clicked what they were for.

'How exactly can you call me your domme when you are constantly telling me what to do and when to do it?' Elsha asked. She wrapped one towel around Julie's eyes, and the world went dark.

'Because I'm willing,' Julie replied, crossing her wrists over her head. 'I'm willing to submit to you.'

Elsha tied her up. 'But only when I do as I'm told?'

This was too much talk. Much too much talk. Julie preferred action over contemplation. That's why she quit school young. That's why she went into general labour. Her body needed to move, it needed to hurt; it required constant sensation, even if that sensation was aching muscles after a 13-hour shift. She loved it. And she loved Elsha. If only the damn girl didn't try her patience so consistently! Elsha was always talk-talk-talking about their relationship, saying Julie had to take it easy or she'd give herself a heart attack some day. Well, that was some day and this was now, and right now she wanted to feel alive in her flesh.

'Would you shut your yap and just cut me, already?'

Elsha tsked as she left the room – Julie could tell by the sound of her swishing skirt that she was walking away. For a split-second, her fingers and toes went numb, and then she panicked. 'Elsha! Elsha? Where are you going? I'm sorry, baby, but you know how I get. I just want it so bad.' No response but shuffling in the next room. 'Come back, Mama. I said some mean things. Come back and punish me, will you?'

The rustle of a long skirt announced Elsha's returned. 'I'm not going to cut you with a knife,' she said, each word slow and measured.

'That's fine,' Julie sputtered. Her heart leapt in her chest. 'You're doling out the punishment, Mama Bear. It's whatever you see fit.'

'Kitchen knives are unsanitary,' Elsha went on. As she spoke, a sound like cracking plastic shot through the room.

Blindfolded, Julie had little sense of where Elsha was standing. She squirmed on the couch, rubbing her thighs together in hopes of getting off a little on the pressure.

'What are you up to?' she asked when all she could hear was a slight flicking sound from somewhere in the room.

'I won't cut you with a knife,' Elsha repeated. Her speech was tortoise-slow. She drew out every syllable, and it made Julie crazy. 'The last thing I want is for you to get an infection. Real cutters use razor blades. Didn't you know that?'

As she stared into the microcosm of stars swirling before he eyes, Julie's mind reeled. Was Elsha going to do it? 'No, I didn't know that,' she said. 'How did *you* know that?'

Elsha's skirt swished until Julie could feel her looming over the couch. 'Saw it on TV. You'd learn a lot if you'd only watch a documentary or two between your police dramas.'

An icy rectangle met her belly. It was metal – that much, Julie could tell. She knew what it must be, but still asked, 'What's that?'

'That's the blade,' Elsha said. 'You crack open a new safety razor and take out the blade. It's sterile. That's what you cut with.'

Julie could feel her pussy drooling in anticipation. Her muscles throbbed for action. 'Do it,' she said. Above her head, her hands started to tremble. She'd grab that razor blade herself if Elsha didn't get a move on. 'Cut me. Come on, just grab the thing and fucking do it, already!'

The blade seemed to bounce on her stomach as she writhed, but Elsha removed it before it could do any harm. 'Patience,' she said in a whisper. 'The waiting is the best part, Julie. You're impetuous, you're rash, and you speak out of turn.' The more Elsha said, the softer she spoke, until it was a strain to make out her words. 'If you want me to hurt you, to cut you, you must be willing to wait.'

But Julie wasn't willing. Her body screamed for the pain. 'Just do it. I need it now.'

Elsha's skirt met the loveseat with a soft thump.

'Don't fucking sit down, you ...' Julie didn't call her a

128

bitch. That wouldn't have helped her case. 'Get over here and cut me up!'

Elsha switched on the radio and scanned until she found a classical music station. 'Ah, Debussy! Don't you love his impressionistic composition style? It's so soothing.'

'God!' Julie cried as she writhed on the couch. There was nothing keeping her in the room. She could have gotten up and left ... but then there was no chance Elsha would take the blade to her flesh. Elsha was the cruellest of dommes. She always made Julie wait. And Julie had no patience.

But Elsha was right in one regard – the music on the radio calmed Julie down. Her heart stopped palpitating. Her muscles relaxed. Staring into the darkness of her blindfold, she breathed at a normal rate until she felt the base of the settee sink slightly under Elsha's weight. Then, all bets were off. 'Do it,' she said. 'Cut me up, Mama Bear.' The tension returned to her muscles, and she grasped the loose ends of the tea towel securing her wrists.

'Are you absolutely certain?' Elsha asked.

Julie breathed out hard. 'Yes! Haven't I said it, like, 40 times? Yes!'

She felt the blade resting against her skin, right at the base of her bellybutton. If she bucked up, the razor would pierce her flesh all at once, and she thought about doing it, but in truth, she was afraid. She wouldn't be able to see how deep it'd gone in, or how much she was bleeding. So she gave control over to Elsha, if only in her mind.

Elsha pushed the blade down until it sliced through her skin. At first, it didn't hurt at all. The pain didn't kick in until she dragged it slowly down Julie's belly. Her muscles were paralysed with fear. She couldn't budge, even as Elsha positioned herself between Julie's open legs.

'Is it bleeding?' Julie finally asked. She wasn't sure she wanted to hear the answer.

Setting a warm palm flat against her pussy, Elsha said, 'No, I didn't go too deep the first time. Want me to do it again?'

Trepidation gripped Julie by the throat, and still she stammered, 'Go deep.'

Elsha held her body still while she pressed the blade to the base of Julie's navel and slit her belly open. She gasped – a desperate sort of wheezing gasp. 'Damn it!' she cried before diving at Julie's stomach and pressing her tongue to it.

'Oh my God!' Julie cringed in response to Elsha's reaction. 'What did you do? Am I bleeding?'

'You're bleeding,' Elsha said, licking the length of her belly again and again.

'Is it bad?'

Pressing her palm to the wound, Elsha squeezed Julie's pussy lips together hard and her veins flowed with a confused mix of pleasure and anxiety. Still, the fact that Elsha hadn't responded worried her.

'Is it bad?' Julie asked again. The pressure on her belly lifted with Elsha's hand, and now all Julie felt was the sting of the wound and Elsha's fingers as they crept inside her wet pussy. 'Well?'

'It's all right,' Elsha said with a sigh. 'But it's deeper than I'd intended. I went at it too fast. I should have taken my time.'

Julie took a deep breath, which spiked when she felt Elsha's thumb on her clit. It moved in circles, drawing Julie's bud erect as her fingers stroked the depths. 'OK, well ...' Julie's brain was already fried from fear. 'Take your time, then. Christ, I don't want you to fucking kill me.'

As she licked Julie's stomach, Elsha moved her fingers slowly inside her open cunt. Julie felt her body writhing, her breath rising and falling, and her whims take on new fancies as Elsha scored shallow gashes along her side. The pain felt nearly as good as the pleasure. Maybe better. She couldn't yet tell which was more intense.

When Julie raised her hips to greet the circling thumb,

Elsha withdrew from her pussy. She fluttered like a blossom on the wind until her mouth found the "V" of Julie's thighs. Pressing her palm against the major injury along Julie's stomach, she said, 'Some blood trickled down.'

Elsha licked Julie's pussy lips and her whole body shuddered. 'Oh God,' Julie said, her breath flitting from her chest. A bolt of worry shot through her veins. 'I'm bleeding that much?'

Without offering the faintest reply, Elsha sucked her throbbing clit between full lips. Julie thrust without thinking – that was her Pavlovian response to feeling the most sensitive part of her body inside Elsha's warm, wet mouth. The stars in her field of vision swirled off into galaxies as she pressed her pussy in tight circles against Elsha's face. The cuts all over her stomach pinched every time she moved, but the sharp twinges couldn't dissuade her from building pleasure on pain.

Julie planted her feet against the cushions. When she'd lifted her ass far enough off the couch, Elsha dragged some juice down to Julie's asshole and slowly pushed her fingertip inside. That set off Julie's tripwire, and she bucked against Elsha's sucking mouth. Elsha pushed down harder on her stomach as she devoured Julie's clit. Her finger remained steady inside Julie's hole, and her ass-ring gripped and clung to it as the wave took over. She came loud and proud, her body jutting and trembling. Her toes stayed curled even after she'd settled down on the couch. For a moment, all she could do was breathe and mutter, 'Oh God, Mama Bear ...'

Elsha disentangled her body from Julie's and untied her wrists first. 'Do me a favour and press down on your cut while I take off your blindfold.'

As droplets trickled from the edges of her wound, Julie pressed her palm flat against it. The pain had dulled to a subdued ache, but it still felt better when she applied pressure.

'Will you be upset with me if there's a scar?'

Julie's heart trembled. This sort of play always made her feel happy, unified and bonded with her girl. 'Why would I be upset with you?' she chuckled. 'It was *my* idea, for Christ's sake!'

'I know,' Elsha replied. The moment she'd removed the makeshift blindfold, Julie's gaze darted to her belly. She lifted her hand to check out the damage. But there was none. She looked back and forth between her stomach and her hand, looking for any sign of blood. Nothing. No sign of cuts or scratches, and the razor blade rested clean on the glass tabletop.

Tossing the tea towels over her shoulder, Elsha offered a mischievous grin. She stuck out her pinkie finger to show Julie its long, sharp nail. Before Julie could think how to respond, Elsha pressed the nail to the underside of her arm and dragged it down the length.

'Jesus fuck!' Julie cried, grasping the new wound. 'That hurts like hell.' Of course, there was no cut. Elsha's fingernail didn't even leave a red mark in its wake.

Elsha loomed like a cunning fox over her. 'If you want to be my sub,' she said, 'I'm going to dominate you my way.'

The Next Step
by Jeanette Grey

One little step.

All Cynthia had to do was take one little step, and she would be out her front door. From there, she knew that she could do this. Breathing deeply, she lifted her foot and tugged at the door, poised just at the cusp of moving forward. But then, at the very last moment, she froze, her chest seizing painfully.

With a sigh, Cynthia took her hand off the knob and retreated back a little farther into the shadows of the entryway. The foyer to her building was small and dim, and for all that it was public, it was safe. Comfortable.

Nothing else about Cynthia's situation was comfortable right now.

Biting her lip, she inched forward again, emerging just far enough into the light to be able to see herself reflected in one of the panes of glass that framed the door. She looked good, she knew, but it almost made things worse to acknowledge it. Her hands curled up into fists, and for a moment, as she contemplated yet again the single step she needed to take, her stomach clenched and twisted.

Cynthia Cohen was not the kind of woman who didn't wear underwear. She wasn't the kind of woman who wore short skirts or knee-high stiletto boots while she was not wearing underwear, and she most certainly was *not* the kind of woman who wore her metal-studded leather play collar out of the house.

Yet still, here she was, prepared to do all of those things.

For years, Cynthia Cohen would have said that a perfect evening was one spent reading a book on the couch in her living room, her long red hair twisted into a bun and secured with chopsticks, her feet toasty in fuzzy slippers and her curves disguised by baggy pyjamas.

But then she had met Richard, and Richard had helped her to see that an even more perfect evening included being naked and sweaty, her hands bound. On her knees.

Just the thought of their nights spent together in such a fashion made Cynthia's throat tight and her chest hot, the aching space between her thighs clenching uncomfortably. As her lover, Richard had helped her to see herself as more than the quiet bookworm she had always been. But it was as her master that he had helped her to explore what it was to be a sexual woman – to give and to submit. To serve and to let go.

To receive.

When he had first revealed his preferences for rougher, kinkier sex, she had been wary, of course. No one had been more surprised than she when she'd realised just how much the way he tugged her hair and ordered her around turned her on. Slowly, over a period of months, she had given herself over to his desires, finding that the more she pleased him, the more she pleased herself. That she liked being a sexual creature. An object.

A toy.

Still paralysed at the threshold to the door, Cynthia shivered as she thought about the kind of toy Master increasingly seemed to want her to be. In their more tender moments, he had explained his desire to help her see herself as a beautiful, sensual woman. It was one of her last few boundaries – her reluctance to allow herself to behave wantonly anywhere outside of the bedroom or the playroom.

As her lover, he had begged her to eschew her librarian

glasses and her frumpy sweaters.

Finally, as her master, he had ordered her to.

The memory of his voice, rough and lustful in her ear as he'd explained what he wanted her to do, awakened another blooming rush of desire inside her body and, with a deep breath, she squared her shoulders and brought her hand up to touch her collar. The feeling of leather and metal beneath her fingertips helped to ground her, and she finally found the frame of mind she needed to do what had been asked of her.

She opened the door.

And stepped through.

Cynthia made it about half a block before she realised exactly how wrong she had been, huddling in her entryway and trying to summon the courage to move. Yes, the first step had been the most difficult one, but it had hardly been the only one that would challenge her.

The fact of the matter was that her feet hurt and a bitter winter wind was whipping up her obscenely short skirt, making the bare flesh of her thighs feel numb from the chill. She was still on a side street, and already she had passed half a dozen people, their eyes flashing with equal parts judgement and lust by turns, and she couldn't tell which one bothered her more.

Or which one aroused her more.

The combination of excitement and trepidation was beginning to overwhelm her as she continued down the street. When she felt her breath begin to catch at all the warring feelings welling up inside her, she forced herself to walk more slowly, one shaky hand coming up to rest on her heart, her fingertips sliding along the edge of her collar, reminding her who she was and why she was doing this.

Reminding her of her master.

Reminding her that while she could never have done something like this for herself, she could do it for him.

She could be his beautiful, sexy, dirty girl.

She could do it because he wanted her to.

By the time she made it to the train station, the pain in her feet had subsided into a low, deep ache, much like the one she often bore from her master's spankings, and between that and the constriction of her collar around her neck, she was beginning to truly fall into the headspace she'd just begun to grasp on her way out the door. Slowly, as she walked up to the turnstile, she could feel things growing both sharper and fuzzier in her mind.

In her head, she could hear her master's voice, calling her a slut as he fucked her into the bed. In the lustful, damning gazes of the men and women around her, Cynthia *felt* like a slut.

Only, unlike the shameful feeling she had expected to accompany those stares, she felt powerful. She felt sexy and alive.

She felt like the kind of girl who could not only walk through a crowded train station without panties, but one who could sink to her knees there on the grimy floor and take her master's cock inside her throat, sucking him down and making him come while all the world looked on.

Emboldened, Cynthia moved through the station with a sense of purpose, her hips swaying and her chest jutting out more proudly. Her hard nipples were increasingly sensitive as they rubbed against her shirt, every motion sending another thrilling rush of warmth to the space between her thighs. When the edge of her skirt caught on the turnstile, she felt the cold rush of air over her ass, and she flushed even more deeply at the knowledge that she was probably flashing everybody. In her head, she could imagine all the people staring at her bare flesh, her eyes darting to the fronts of trousers that were tightening just looking at her.

By the time she reached the platform, her thighs were slick, her sex swollen, and she found herself shifting uncomfortably from one foot to the other as she waited for the train. Per her instructions, she stood at the very edge of

136

the platform, right where the last car would soon be pulling in. All around her, people continued to fill in the spaces and, with a tingle of anticipation, she recognised that the train would be full.

That soon, she would be amid a throng of bodies, encased in their heat, with nothing standing in the way of any stranger's roaming hand and her flesh.

A rush of warm air bombarded her, pulling her from her thoughts as the roar of wheels on steel drowned out all of the surrounding voices. Her skirt was pressed against her thighs, riding up dangerously high with the force of the wind created by the train. As if on cue, the moment the hem drew up to flutter across her pussy, the doors of the last car slid open in front of her, and she was left burning beneath the stare of a half dozen people, all casting lascivious, judging gazes down her form.

Sucking in a deep breath, Cynthia met each pair of eyes and stepped up onto the train. Bodies parted to make way for her, but she still felt her sides being brushed as she reached forward to grab onto the pole. There were a couple of open places to sit in the filling car, but her master had told her to stand, so she stood, her hips pressing to the half wall between the aisle and the first row of seats, her knuckles white as they clung on.

As it roared back to life, the lurching motion of the train sent another thrill through Cynthia's body, and she moved with it, swaying with every turn, vibrating with the heady rush of turning wheels. At every stop, more and more people filtered into the car, and it wasn't long until she felt the crush of heat she had anticipated, bodies all around her.

Then there was a touch – a hand dragging over fabric, rough fingertips on overheated thighs.

She was ready to panic, her whole body tensing and her mind finally returning to rationality, reminding her that she was not that type of woman. That this was wrong.

But then the man behind her spoke.

'You must be fucking soaked, dirty girl. I can practically smell you from here.'

Master.

The deep, gravelly voice at her ear relaxed her instantly, and suddenly instead of tensing and pulling away, Cynthia let herself fall back, the relief of a warm, broad chest against her spine reassuring her in every possible way.

'Did you miss me, baby? Or were you too busy being eye-fucked by every man on this train?'

She tried to turn, but his hand clamped down on her thigh, the other one coming up to squeeze her waist. 'Uh-uh,' he chastised her. 'You keep those pretty eyes facing forward while I touch you.'

Melting at his command, she felt her vision glaze over, another wet rush of warmth flooding her pussy as the hand on her thigh dragged higher up, lifting her skirt. Her master's body behind her and the half-wall in front of her blocked what was happening from the other passengers' view, but she felt like they had to know. Wasn't it obvious from the way she panted? From the way her eyes were glazed and her cheeks flushed?

If it was, she didn't have much time to contemplate it. Hot breath pushed past her ear, making her eyes fall closed with the eroticism of being touched this way, here in the middle of a crowded train car.

'Now I believe I asked you a question,' the voice continued.

Her answer was a breathy moan. 'Of course I missed you, Master.'

'I'm glad to hear that, Pet. Though I don't think you missed me nearly enough. Not if this sloppy cunt of yours is any indication.' His hand moved up the back of her thigh, and she instinctively spread her legs as his fingertips brushed over her lips. 'Come now, feel for yourself.'

Cynthia shivered when Master directed her hand beneath her skirt, shifting them closer to the side of the car as people exited and entered. Once they were more safely tucked into a corner, she obeyed. Dipping her hand beneath the edge of her skirt, she swiped her fingertips through her swollen lips, drawing just one circle over the needy flesh of her clit.

'Taste yourself.'

Her fingers bore the sweet-salt-tang of sex as she discreetly flicked her tongue over them. It wasn't a taste she relished, but she knew how much it turned her master on when she licked herself from her fingers.

'Does it taste good?' he breathed in her ear, his voice so quiet that even she could barely hear him over the roar of the train. 'Does my little slut like tasting how bad she wants it?'

Cynthia turned her head to whisper over her shoulder, 'She likes tasting you better.'

At that, he finally leant forward, pulling his hand away to make room for his hips, the hard line of his cock pressing against her ass. 'That might be able to be arranged,' he murmured, sucking softly at the tender skin of her neck. 'What do you think, Pet? Want to suck me? Right here? Right now?'

She shuddered hard, one hand coming up to press flat against the wall in front of her as her knees threatened to give out. 'If you want me to,' she finally answered, the desperate arousal clear in her voice.

'Such a good little slut,' he murmured, kissing all up and down her neck and holding her so that her ass was flush with his hips. 'So eager to please, aren't you?'

'Yes,' she breathed.

'Maybe I should take you up on that. You have the best fucking mouth.' His fingers closed more tightly around her waist, and she felt her abdomen twist with both desire and nerves. Pulled slightly from their game, she revisited the limits they'd discussed a few nights earlier. While she'd agreed to sex in public, it had been with the condition that he would only ask under circumstances with minimal risk of getting caught.

She trusted him implicitly, but still, there was a thin trickle of fear that he might push her. That the next step in their journey might be too big entirely.

'Calm down, Pet,' he whispered. In spite of his still-gruff tone, his thumb began to rub reassuring circles against her hip. 'Look around.'

Trying to catch her breath, Cynthia did just that, letting her eyes really focus on what was happening around them. She startled at how empty the car seemed now, compared with how it had been when she'd boarded. Searching the blur of brick and darkness rushing past the windows, she finally recognised that they were well past downtown and heading toward the end of the line.

That soon the train would grow emptier still.

Her mouth formed a little "O" in her surprise, eliciting a chuckle from behind her. 'You see, love?'

She nodded and sucked in a deep breath that finally seemed to fill her lungs. 'Yes, Master.'

'Good girl.' His fingertips ghosted up her spine before coming to rest just below her collar. The train slowed, screeching to a stop at a station Cynthia knew well, and she watched another handful of people disembark, connecting eyes with one man whose gaze lingered on her tits as he made his way to the door.

Master's eyes were directed elsewhere, though. Nudging her jaw, he directed her to look to the back of the car and the now-empty bench that faced the rear window, just behind another divider wall. 'Ah, good. It looks like our seat is available.' Almost peeling her from the wall, he guided her down the aisle, steadying her against the rocking motion of the train as it picked up speed.

Stopping, he paused and pushed her to the side, brushing against her body as he slid past her and into the seat. It was the first time she'd actually seen him all night, and her chest squeezed at the sight of him, as handsome and dapper as ever in a pale grey suit and tie beneath his trench coat. The look on his face was intense and lustful, but fully in command as he pulled off his coat and motioned for her to sit on his lap.

His body was warm beneath her as she settled atop his thighs, her back to his chest, and she was instantly comforted by the way he closed his arms around her, draping the coat across her shoulders and arranging it to cover her. She could feel his cock, hard and insistent against her ass, and the approving groan that slipped through his lips as she pushed against it made her sex clench.

'You like that, do you?' he asked. 'Take it out, then. Feel it.'

Her nerves fluttered again as she moved to follow his instructions. 'Shh,' he whispered. Sensing her anxiety, he brought his fingertips to stroke the edge of her collar in a reassuring gesture that was also a reminder. A warning even. 'Trust me.'

Swallowing, she did. Opening his fly and sliding a hand into his boxers, she finally found the hot swollen flesh that she'd been craving, her thumb slipping through the slickness at the head of it. His hand brushed hers away, and he pushed the fabric of her skirt up as he pulled her back against him. At the feeling of his cock against her backside, she whimpered with lust and anxiety, each feeding the other until she was a raw line of need.

'Do you feel how hard you make me? How much I love seeing you all dressed up like this for me?' He ground against her slowly as he spoke, the slightest flexing of his hips pushing his cock to the flesh of her ass. 'Knowing I have the sexiest woman in the world pressed against me, ready to please me?'

Cynthia exhaled roughly and nodded. 'Yes.'

'Go on then,' he breathed.

Closing her eyes, she hesitated for just a moment, but she knew she wanted this. She was ready to please him.

She trusted him.

Lifting her hips, she felt the head of his cock slide up the length of her slit, pushing tantalizingly against her clit before retreating to rest, thick and full, at her opening. She sat back down with a low whine of pleasure, feeling every inch as he slid inside, filling and stretching.

'Such a good little cunt,' he grunted as their thighs met, his body fully seated inside hers. 'So good wrapped around my cock.'

'Yes,' she breathed. 'Please.'

'Go ahead. Slowly.' As she began to slide up and down his length, he kept one hand on her hip and the other on her shoulder. Every time she rose, he pushed back down, keeping her strokes shallow and subtle, and she felt a pressing warmth inside her chest, knowing that her trust was not unfounded.

'Do you know how sexy this is?' he asked gruffly as he slid home again. 'Fucking you like this? Here on a train? Knowing anyone could catch us with me balls-deep inside you?'

She groaned wantonly in response, his voice exciting her almost as much as his cock, and she could already feel the edges of oblivion as the fire grew between her thighs.

'Anyone could be looking at us right now, Pet. But they have no idea what's going on. Only you and I know. Just us.'

Writhing and panting, she worked herself over him, her back arching until he began to press against the electric spot within her with every stroke. 'I love fucking you, Master,' she whimpered. 'Only you.'

'Yes, Pet,' he groaned. 'Put your hand on that pretty little pussy of yours. Make yourself come.'

She obeyed immediately, rubbing her clit in quick circles. Only, as she began to approach the precipice, she heard the scratchy static of the train's loudspeaker cracking to life.

'Next stop is 95th Street Station. All passengers must exit the train at 95th Street Station.'

Cynthia groaned in protest and in frustration, hastening the motion of her hand as her master bit down on her neck. 'Now,' he growled, licking a long stripe up to her ear. A few short thrusts later, she could finally see the edge, and she let the sensation overwhelm her, warmth bursting out and through her as she exploded in the kind of climax she could feel in her toes and in her throat.

'Fuck,' Master grunted, pulling her up until he could fuck her freely from beneath her, pushing into her a half dozen more times before he tensed and cursed, sending a rush of liquid warm through her sex as he spilled and shuddered.

The next few minutes were a blur for Cynthia. Overwhelmed and still quaking with sensation, she was aware of someone approaching their seat, of Richard pulling out of her and securing his coat around her shoulders, helping her up and cradling her against his side as he urged her up and off the train. Somehow, she made it to the top of the stairs where he allowed her to pause for a moment, holding her and kissing her temple, telling her what a good girl she was and how much he loved her. How proud he was of her.

All she could do was laugh.

The wind outside was biting, but less so than before, bundled as she was and cloaked in her lover's smell. With the sort of warm, brisk efficiency she loved him for, he bustled her into a taxi, pulling her against his side as he instructed the driver to take them home. She could feel his hands on her face, tilting it up, where she met concerned eyes and a grim, firm mouth.

'Are you all right, darling?'

'Fine,' she mumbled sleepily. With a contented sigh, she dropped her head back to his shoulder and grinned lazily. 'Great, actually.'

The worry slowly ebbed from Richard's posture, and he laughed against her ear. 'Welcome back,' he murmured as he stroked her hair.

'Never left.'

'Yes, you did, love.' His hand parted the edges of the coat and he rubbed the flimsy material of her skirt between his fingers. 'Hell, Cynthia. You left the house. In just this.'

She shrugged. 'You told me to.'

'Yes,' he agreed. 'But somehow I never expected you to do it.'

She was suddenly much more alert as she registered his words, sitting up straighter. 'Did you not want me to?'

He rolled his eyes and bent to kiss her mouth for the first time all day. 'Of course I did, silly girl. I was just trying to be realistic.' Pursing his lips, he pulled back to look at her. 'You seemed so against it. I'm just curious what changed.'

She thought about it for a moment, letting her eyes drift to the windows of the taxi and the city streets rushing by. The whole experience had been beyond sexy, and it had made her feel even more powerful than she could have imagined a few short hours earlier, fretting endlessly in the foyer to their building, trying to summon the courage to follow through.

The image she had seen of herself in the glass floated up in her mind at the same time as her eyes focused on her face reflected in the window of the cab. Both images were of a woman so divorced from who Cynthia was, most days.

But they were still her.

'I just decided, I guess,' she finally answered.

'Decided what?'

'That I could be both.' She lifted her hand to his cheek as she spoke, rubbing it gently and feeling his smile beneath her fingers. 'That I could be your dirty girl and still be me.'

'Oh, honey,' he said, pressing his lips once more to hers. 'You always were.' He grinned more brightly. 'And you always will be.'

At that, she nodded and averted her gaze, burying her face against his neck and blushing deeply.

Sure, she had been nervous initially. But now, basking in

the afterglow, she could scarcely remember why.

Now, all she could focus on was what her master would ask of her next.

And she couldn't wait to find out what the next step in her journey would be.

The Initiation of Lily
by Angel Propps

The dungeon was a small one, known only to a handful of women. It lay at the foot of a set of stairs that hid behind a door in a small and perfectly ordinary house that sat in a slightly seedy neighbourhood populated by mostly older people and younger couples with small children who could often be seen during the day running about on the playground that the house sat across a shaded street from.

It was night and the kids were all gone, the playground was dark and the neighbourhood quiet. Through the fog and darkness amber-coloured headlights could be seen pulling up to the curb and into the driveway of the house. Footsteps came up the rickety back stairs; some thudding and heavy in 50s hood-style boots, some clicking and tapping as the slender heels the owners of those feet wore pranced showily up the steps. Some registered not as all because they were bare and they tramped into the house leaving toe prints and grass flecks on the tiled and none-too-clean kitchen floor.

Kisses were exchanged and laughter rang out. Coats were dropped off shoulders to reveal latex, leather or naked bodies below. More talk swirled through the crowded upper rooms as the footsteps continued to come up those stairs and every set brought a fresh tensing of muscles, a fresh sense of anticipation. Leather creaked. Bags jangled and clattered in ominous and yet happy tones as they were set on the tired carpet of the living room floor.

A nylon string guitar rested on top of a closed and neglected upright piano, a careless hand struck the wooden cover and an eddy of dust spun madly; this caused a woman with pretty red hair, oddly light green eyes and a colourful tattoo on her bare back and right shoulder to sneeze. On the worm-eaten wood of the coffee table one platter sat filled with fruit, another held crackers and an assortment of cheese and small fat bowls filled with foil-wrapped chocolates, but few of the women took any. They mostly held their glasses of sparkling water or sodas and waited.

That they were waiting for something was obvious. The anticipation hung in the air. It crackled with the same high tension that accompanied heat lightning. At that moment they were flash without fire and they knew it. They knew it and they were waiting, waiting for the spark, waiting for ignition.

There was a final stamp of heavy boots on the boards. The room grew thick with a tangible sexual tension. A woman with skin the colour of a rare pearl and a thick brown brush of pubic hair swallowed hard as she tried to wipe away the trickling moisture from her naked thighs before it could betray her excitement.

The back door opened into the kitchen with its familiar squeal of rusted hinge. A current ran through the room and a young girl in a plaid skirt, red bra, black thigh-high fishnets and stilettos quivered once, her body shuddering like the electricity in the room had somehow managed to light her nervous system with its blue pulse.

The woman coming through the door had won the keys to the dungeon years before in a nasty game that was still talked about by the core group. The newcomers they recruited often did not believe the tale: it was too fantastic, too bizarre and, yes, even too disgusting for their newbie ears and tastes.

The young girl in the plaid skirt shivered when she saw her. She was older, in her 50s and her face showed it. Her hair was greying, parted severely in the middle and pulled back sharply from her face in a long braid. Her eyes had drooped and grown reddened over the years, but their odd slate and icy hue had not faded at all, nor had the gleeful sadism that lurked within those depths.

'And you are Lily.'

Lily swallowed hard at the woman's words. It had been explained to her by the girl who had brought her and who was standing nearby that the woman in front of her was allowed anyone and whatever she wanted in the dungeon. Because of that game. It had also been explained to her that the woman was a stone butch who did not play in public and, if she chose her, she would be taken elsewhere.

Jessie knew the girl was afraid and that excited her but she saw the way the girl's eyes kept flickering to Karen, the owner of the dungeon and a femme top with long black hair that had a solid white streak running through it. The girl's eyes kept touching on Karen's leather pants, low-cut top and the rounded mounds of her breasts that shoved at their bare coverings. Jessie knew she would be within her rights to take the girl. She also knew the girl would remember for ever her first night in the dungeon and that she should be allowed what she wanted. When Jessie stepped forward she heard the collective intake of breath all around her. She was there to open the door and to mark the alpha femme *catch du jour*. The night's play hung in the balance; the mood of the entire night would be set by that ceremonial opening.

If she kissed the girl on her cheek or forehead she would be free to play with any of the tops in the room, if she flicked her with her whip the girl would be hers. All eyes were on her and Jessie felt pride swell her chest under her creaking 30-year-old leather jacket as she leant forward and lightly kissed the girl's smooth cheek. The kiss was gentle, the feel of the girl's skin a bare promise of what could have been as Jessie stepped away. She felt an instant pang at the missed opportunity but she knew that a big part of being a great domme was knowing when to let go.

Lily let out a long slow breath as she felt those lips touch her cheek and then move away. She felt her fear slide into something darker and far more seductive as Jessie went to the door, took out the keys and unbolted the locks. The darkness yawned below the door, stretching away into the dungeon.

The women went down the stairs, making the old boards rattle and rumble as they went and Lily felt the first cool breath of understanding blow against her fevered skin as she was taken by the hand by the petite and beautiful redhead who had sneezed at the piano's small dust storm. She gave Lily a beatific smile and said, 'You are the alpha femme tonight. All subs get to choose who tops us but you get first pick tonight. I know you are new so, remember, you get to say no to anything you don't want to do and you are giving a gift so precious that it is beyond compare. Pick wisely and enjoy.' Then she kissed Lily's cold cheek and stepped away.

Lily stood there looking at the women arrayed in a loose circle in front of her. There was Jessie with her hard line of lip and lean hips. Karen and her sexy display of skin. The redheaded femme and the gorgeous light-skinned black woman with the shaved head and round arms and tits shown to perfect advantage in a black leather top. There was an older woman dressed in lingerie. Two butches who were a married couple. Both of them were hard and thick, dressed in matching leather and with their short hair sticking up into messy points. There was another older woman, sweet faced and wide hipped with a sexy round belly and tattoos all down her arms. A young woman with skin so pale she looked like she had been cast from a quarry's purest marble whose only clothing was a pair of long striped stockings. Several other women stood around in the dim lighting and Lily looked at them all.

Lily's eyes kept twitching back to Karen and, finally, she raised a shaking hand and whispered, 'Umm ... could I please ...?' and then she fell silent.

Karen had to turn her head so the girl would not see her crimson-tinted lips cant up in a smile. She fought her glee down and then she asked, 'What do you want?'

Lily had given that a lot of thought. Her eyes went to Sara, the young girl with the marble complexion. They had met at a comic-book store and then became lovers briefly. Sara had begun teaching her about the world of BDSM and the education had struck a deep chord inside Lily. When she had asked her to come to the dungeon she had not had to ask twice and now she gave Lily an encouraging smile and a nod, imparting courage. She had informed Lily which women shared a liking for the particular little kink that made Lily melting hot at the very thought and all Lily had to do was ask. It was the simplest thing. Which is why it was so very hard to do. When Lily spoke her voice was a thick-throated murmur while she described what she wanted, gave Karen her safe word and stood waiting to see if her dream scene would be played out.

'Then come to me, bitch,' Karen said and Lily looked at her, at the women all watching her and back at Sara. She had known this moment would come, had known she would be asked to do this, to prove her willingness to give that precious gift of her submission and she took a long breath ... a longer one ... then she slowly lowered herself to the cold grey floor. When her knees were on the concrete she bent herself forward and began to crawl.

Lily felt the flush and the sense of flying come creeping over her. Her knees scraped concrete and a small stinging burn arose from her skin and she marked it with a quivering sigh. Her nipples tightened and she could feel moisture running from her pussy, soaking into the fabric of her panties.

Karen showed none of her excitement. When Lily got to

her she stuck a booted foot out and, in a bit of ruthlessness, she pushed the young woman's face into the floor. 'I don't think you want it,' she announced and Lily gasped as her skin went first red hot and then ice cold. To her utter surprise she burst into long hard sobs.

'I do want it,' she wept out, 'Please, mistress, please ma'am, I want it so bad ...' And she did. She wanted the things that she had sensed in the small spankings and milder forms of play Sara had shared with her, she wanted to be used, wanted to be fucked. Fucked hard and deep and for hours. She wanted to beg and be punished and she did the only thing she could think of to show how much she wanted all those things. She put her head on those boots and licked them lovingly, the taste of leather filling her mouth and a steady beat of sheer decadent need filling her lower belly.

The domme yanked her up, her hands tangling into hair, the muscles in her arms bunching as she dragged the new sub to her feet and then to a spanking bench set against one wall. Lily was shaking everywhere, her pussy was getting wetter with every sob and she had not one idea why she was crying; she only knew that it felt good and that the woman standing over her seemed to like it.

Karen did like it. She loved to see tears, loved to bring a woman to them and she was well pleased already with this sweet young thing that had stumbled into their dungeon. She shoved Lily face down over the bench. Both women's hormones were raging, their adrenaline climbing higher. Lily shivered as her skirt was removed and her panties were yanked to her knees. A hand slid unapologetically between her ass cheeks, slid down and then fingers shoved brutally inside her cunt. She moaned and whimpered as those digits ground deeply into her, slammed against her walls and then withdrew just as suddenly, leaving a slick trail leaking down her thighs.

'You belong to me,' Karen taunted. 'I can do anything I want to you and I want to turn that hot little ass a really

152

pretty rosy red.'

Karen began the spanking with light slaps, watching the round globes of ass jiggle and ripple as they landed. She was warming up and the sobs and whimpers coming from Lily were exciting her greatly. Her hands grew warm as she spanked and she could feel the heat coming from those ass cheeks; that heat made an answering heat bloom and grow in her pussy. Her breath began to come faster and she finished the spanking with a fast series of slaps so sharp they raised finger-shaped lines across that ass above the already reddened skin.

Lily was sobbing. The pain was there, under the surface. Above it was a lust so intense she felt like she would die if she did not get some relief from it – and soon. Her wet pussy was open and exposed and the cool air of the dungeon blew over it, making her tremble and whimper. During the spanking she had been helplessly arching her ass upwards and into the slaps, not knowing or caring that the reaction was pleasing Karen, not knowing or caring that that reaction marked her as a sub and that she was being observed closely by the others in the dungeon.

Karen slid a pair of latex gloves onto her hands and stripped her leather pants off. She reached into her bag and pulled out the harness. The scent of it – leather and old come that no amount of washing could truly eradicate – making her nipples contract to hard points. She loved the way that cock looked on her. She loved the contrast between womanly curves and hard cock, the way it was so totally outside the norm. The power it imparted to her.

What she really wanted was to totally humiliate the young woman straddling the bench, but it was her first time and so it had to be a softer experience. Karen yanked the sub up, relishing the way she squealed and moaned when she was brought to her feet. The panties were yanked off and Lily wept as she was forced back to her knees and the enormous cock that Karen had fitted into her harness was

153

unceremoniously shoved into her mouth.

'That's right,' Karen snarled. 'Get it all wet, bitch. You wanna make sure that it is 'cause it is going all the way in that tight fucking cunt of yours. I am going to spread that fucking hole wide open with this dick and you better be able to take it all.'

Lily gagged and screamed around the cock. She had to fight for air and her jaw felt like it was going to break from the strain. Her mouth was opened so wide that drool pooled and ran down her chin, sliding down her neck and onto her red bra.

'Suck it,' Karen yelled and slapped that pretty face twice, right cheek, then left. To be cruel, she shoved herself in as hard as she could, arching her hips and back, holding that hair so that the sub could not escape and waiting until she was positive the girl would throw up if she was not given some relief before she withdrew.

Lily was awash with lust and stressed to her limits. Her fight or flight instinct was at its maximum level and her pussy was soaked with her fluids; indeed, they flowed from her and puddled on the floor below her. Her whole body was fighting itself. Her mind was also at war. Society had taught her to accept punishment but reject violence, a laughable notion under any circumstances, and her belief system was being tested to its limits. She took a deep breath and let go, let all of her thoughts and fears slip away and then there was nothing left but the utter sensation of it all. She went into sub space with a scream of release trapped behind the cock the domme was forcing her to accept.

Karen knew when she went all the way under and she found herself able to go higher as a result. Her mind became more focused, more alert. Her body tingled with sex and desire while her mind stood at a distance and judged the scene and its happenings with the coolness of a general watching a battle from a far hillside.

She pulled the cock from Lily's mouth a final time,

watching as the sub crumpled into the floor with her eyes dazed and her moans ringing out loudly. Karen did not give her a long pause – she wanted to keep her deep in space so she pushed her downwards so that she was bent over her knees with her ass in the air and her forehead pressed into the floor.

Karen bound her rapidly and expertly. She pulled Lily's arms behind her, binding them behind her thighs so that she could not move them at all. Lily sobbed and groaned as Karen slid her fingers inside her pussy again, slamming into her wetness. When Lily began to buck and arch Karen administered a hard slap to each ass cheek.

'Do not move until I tell you to,' she ordered. 'Do you fucking understand me?'

'Yes, ma'am,' Lily snivelled.

Karen placed the vibrator on Lily's clit and then she taped it into place, running the bondage tape around Lily's hips to prevent the vibrator from slipping. Lily screamed in pleasure when that powerful purring began humming against her swollen, aching clit.

The cock came in on a wave of pleasure that brought pain with it. It was large and it hurt and Lily screamed even as she bucked backwards in a desperate attempt to get more. Karen retaliated by pulling completely out of her and asking, 'What are you doing? Who said you could move?'

'Nobody,' Lily sobbed. 'Oh please ... please I will be good. I will be *so* good, mistress, please ... please will you fuck me?'

Karen could feel her own clit aching with the need to come. The base of the cock rubbed against her fiercely as she slid back inside the wet pink flesh, watching with a feeling of pure and primitive pleasure as that tunnel opened and spilt beneath her onslaught. She fucked Lily hard, giving her no mercy, just hard and pounding fucking that made the sub beg for more even as she wept and pleaded to come.

'You want to come?' Karen panted out and felt her own orgasm cresting as she spoke. 'You wanna come, you fucking little slut?'

'Yes!' Lily screamed and her body began to pitch helplessly, 'Please ... please ... I want to come on your cock. I want to come – please.'

'Then fucking come,' Karen snarled and her hands lashed out, one of them knotting into a fist that held Lily's hair and yanked her head back and the other slapping at the dusky red ass that was bouncing beneath the force of the fucking.

Lily came. The waves of her orgasm were hard and pulsing, they left her sobbing and screaming in a mixture of pleasure and utter pain. Her knees bled on the floor, her come splashed onto the cock and ran down her already sticky thighs while her heart thundered like a big drum against her chest walls.

A few minutes later Lily wept huge tears while Karen taped a large square sponge into her mouth and forced her back to the floor, shoving her face into the drying and tacky puddles of her come.

'Clean it up,' Karen ordered. 'Clean it all up right now.'

Lily gagged and choked. She burnt red with humiliation and tears dripped down her nose as she cleaned the mess off the floor with her sponge-taped face. When she had cleaned the floor to Karen's satisfaction she was unbound and the scene was brought to an end by the domme sitting her down on a small square rug and rubbing her back and shoulders gently while she asked what about the scene Lily had liked, what she didn't, and if she would do it again.

Around them the woman played, some in extreme and some in sensual ways. Lily looked at bodies writhing and listened to screams and the orgasmic cries and smiled as she said, 'Oh yes. I will be back again. I promise.'

Karen smiled too. She knew she had made the new sub's initiation one to remember. She felt a sudden surge of nostalgia, remembering her own first time. The dungeon hummed with its power. The women lived out their scenes. They changed and shifted reality, made new rules that suited them – gave them a safe space in which to be. It was a form of magic and the dungeon pulsed and breathed with it. The newly initiated watched the other scenes, marking and remembering who liked what and seeing things she knew she would be trying eventually. Jessie watched over them all as she walked the dungeon in her role as monitor. She looked down at Lily and smiled. Lily smiled back and a promise hung shimmering in the air for a moment.

Outside the rain came down and a car slid past the plain and everyday house on the corner that held so much magic, the house that nobody ever looked at twice because it was just so ordinary.

Trust Me
by Jade Melisande

'Trust me,' he said, and brushed a strand of her blonde hair off her forehead. He was staring down into her eyes with an earnestness she was unaccustomed to in her usually light-hearted lover.

Elizabeth smiled uncertainly. 'Of course I trust you,' she replied.

He slid his hands down her arms and grasped her hands in his, then slowly brought them around behind her and held them there. 'No,' he said, 'I mean, "Trust me *now*." To do this.'

She took a sharp breath, unnaturally loud in the sudden stillness of the room. 'Eric–' His hands were firm, but gentle. He stroked his thumbs along the inside of her wrists, where they met each other in his hands. She shivered.

'I know you're afraid,' he said softly. 'But trust me, Elizabeth. I won't hurt you.'

She held herself very still, wanting desperately to pull back against his hands, knowing it was illogical to feel the fear that coursed through her at just that minimal level of confinement – but there it was.

'I–'

He lifted one hand to her cheek, brushed a finger across her lower lip. His eyes, grey green in the morning light, never left hers. '*Trust* me,' he said again.

Of all the things she'd let him do to her in the almost-year they'd been together, she'd never let him pin her, never let him restrain her, could barely tolerate him even holding her wrists above her head. It was irrational, she knew, but she had been unable to shake her terror of it, of being bound in any way. And so he had spanked her, fucked her, slapped her, dripped wax on her, made her scream with orgasms and occasionally with pain, all without once binding her with rope, leather, his hands or restraints of any kind.

A sacrifice to be sure, for this man who loved all things rope, who used leather with abandon, and who loved the feel of a woman helpless beneath his hand.

Still holding her wrists, still holding her gaze, he moved her slowly back until she felt the couch behind her knees. Moving carefully, like one would around a frightened animal that just might bite in its fear, he reached down and picked something up off the sofa. She shuddered as she felt the slide of silk rope on her skin.

'I'm not going to make it tight,' he said. He looked down and began to loop the rope around her wrists. 'This rope won't even hold a good knot. But this isn't about what's here–' he tapped her wrists where he'd looped the rope, 'it's about what's here.' He tapped her temple lightly. 'And here.' Another tap, just over her heart. 'I'm going to take care of you this morning. All morning. And you'll have to trust me to do that.' He stopped what he was doing and looked back into her eyes. 'OK? Can you do that?'

She licked her lips. Felt the sensuous, intoxicating slip of the rope against her skin, felt her own incipient helplessness. She'd never let anyone take care of her, not since she'd left home at 16 to escape her bully of a stepfather; not since she'd seen what a killing-noose dependency was, after her father had passed away and her mother had found herself barely able to function without her husband's direction. She'd quickly remarried another domineering man, the stepfather Elizabeth had run away to escape, and had fallen into the same helpless role with him.

160

Elizabeth looked into Eric's eyes, searching for something, though she wasn't sure what. All she saw there was love and gentleness. This was the man she had let love her in ways she had never imagined, the man she trusted with all her heart. He had never abused that trust, but instead had built on it, day by day. She felt something loosen inside herself, unravelling like the silken ends of a frayed rope. Slowly, her eyes never leaving his, she nodded.

She had arrived at his house after her morning run, still in her work-out clothes, as was her habit on Saturdays. Normally she would run a bath and he would make coffee, then he would sit on a chair by the tub and they would sip coffee and chat while she relaxed and bathed. Now he untied her wrists long enough to pull off her tanktop and sports bra, then retied them behind her back and bent to untie her shoelaces and remove her shoes and socks. With a hand under each arm he helped her to stand, and she stood mutely as he slid her shorts down over her hips and to the floor. He unwound the band that held her hair in a ponytail and ran his fingers through it, tousling it, shaking it out into a curly mass over her shoulders, where it brushed against her naked skin and tickled her. It was an odd sensation, being undressed in this almost-detached way, and yet she felt a tingle of excitement, of arousal, at the efficiency of his hands, cool on her exercise-heated skin; at the thought of being touched by him, in just this way, all morning.

He led her into the kitchen and sat her carefully on a barstool at the breakfast bar. She was surprised at how much she relied on her arms being free for her balance, and was grateful for his close attention to her. Part of her attention stayed on him as he moved around the kitchen, grinding the beans and setting the coffee to brew, but another part was acutely focused on the sensation of the rope around her wrists. It was not loose, but neither did it bite into her skin. Instead it simply held her, firmly, as his hands had done earlier.

She moved her wrists experimentally, and then with more determination, testing the limits of her movement, and felt a brief flash of fear, a tightness in her chest, when she realised she couldn't slide or twist her hands free. She started to genuinely struggle, to panic, her breath coming faster as she twisted her hands this way and that.

And then she felt his hand on her head, felt him stroking her hair, soothing her. She hadn't even realised her eyes were closed, had forgotten his presence in the room. She stilled under his hand, breathing in his scent.

He continued to stroke her, brushing the hair off her forehead and over her shoulders; cupping his fingers around the back of her neck, under her hair, in a gesture made all the more intimate by the fact that she was captured there, hands behind her back, by his rope. Eyes still closed, enjoying the sensations, her breath caught.

His hands continued their soothing of her, stroking down across her shoulders and still further, until he was cupping her breasts in a way that was achingly familiar to her. Familiar, and yet entirely new, with her arms bound. Her nipples tautened beneath his palms and she arched her back unconsciously, thrusting them deeper into his hands, her earlier panic subsided in the surfeit of sensation as he pinched and pulled at her nipples, rolling them between fingers and thumb. She felt his breath against her lips and then he was kissing her, his mouth covering hers as one hand snaked still lower, across her flat belly and to the "V" between her thighs. As his tongue parted her lips and pushed deep into her mouth, his fingers parted her pussy lips and pushed deep into the wetness he found there. Thrusting, dipping, teasing and spreading, his fingers kept time with his mouth and tongue until she was writhing beneath his hands. Just when she thought she could bear it no longer, when she knew she was going to explode in an orgasm–

He stopped. He pulled his mouth away and slid his fingers gently out of her even as she thrust her hips toward him as though to pull them back in. She stared at him stupidly, panting.

'Not yet,' he said against her mouth, before turning away, a glimmer of amusement in his eyes.

'Hungry?' he asked from the stove.

It took her a moment to gather her thoughts. 'I ... um, sure,' she finally said, dumbfounded at the abrupt change in activities, but realising she had no control over how things played out.

'Good,' he said. 'Sit tight and I'll make us some breakfast.'

She watched, bemused, as he bustled around the kitchen, chopping vegetables, heating a frying pan and getting bacon out of the refrigerator. Soon the kitchen was redolent with the scents of bacon frying, sautéing peppers and bread toasting and, above it all, the sharp tang of coffee brewing, deep and dark. She felt her mouth watering.

While the eggs cooked, he got down two mugs and poured coffee into them. He liked his coffee black, but she liked hers thick with flavoured cream and sugar. She watched as he prepared hers, and brought it over to the breakfast bar in front of her.

'Thirsty?' he asked.

She stuck her tongue out at him. 'Nice,' she said. 'Tease me when I can't get a drink.'

He chuckled. 'Lean forward,' he said. Dubiously, she did so. He lifted her mug and blew on its contents. After a moment, he tested it, wrinkling his nose at its sweetness and making her laugh. Then he offered her the lip of the mug. Hesitantly, she leant forward and took a sip. The coffee was sufficiently cooled and very sweet, just the way she liked it. He tilted the cup slowly enough that she could swallow without choking, and fast enough that she didn't feel ungainly, having to gulp at the liquid. Their eyes met over the lip of the cup, and she felt heat course through her that had nothing to do with the coffee warming her. He reached a

hand out and brushed a stray curl from her face and then set
the cup down to return to his cooking.

Moments later he brought a plate over with a giant
omelette and four pieces of toast. He sat next to her, his
body solid and comforting.

'Eric,' she said, when she saw that he meant to feed her.

'Quiet,' he ordered. 'Eat.'

And she did, marvelling at herself for the feeling of
contentment that came over her as she allowed him to fork
bitefuls of egg, bacon and cheese between her lips, as he
brought a napkin to her mouth to wipe toast crumbs away, as
he offered her more coffee. She was overwhelmed by the
intimacy of such careful attention to every detail, but also
achingly aware of him physically; of his fingers brushing
her lips, the chafe of his jeans against her bare skin (he had
not undressed when he had taken off her clothes), of the heat
that crackled between them. Her skin felt electric, attuned to
his touch, even as she felt strangely shy, being naked and
bound while he remained clothed and free.

Finally, he stood and took their plates to the sink.

'OK,' he said, after rinsing the dishes. 'Bath time.'

She frowned as he went into the bathroom.

'What are you doing?' she called to him.

He poked his head around the bathroom door and raised
an eyebrow at her. 'I should think that would be obvious,'
he said. 'Running you a bath.'

'But ...' She made a gesture with her bound wrists.

He walked over to her, helped her to her feet and into the
bathroom. 'You're going to trust me, right?'

She swallowed, looked at the rapidly filling tub; nodded
uncertainly.

He guided her to the edge of the tub. 'Well?' he said.

She stood at the edge for several minutes, then glanced at
him again, wondering if he really meant to do this. She took
a shallow breath, then another deeper one, willing herself to
be calm. All the while, he waited patiently, watching her.

Finally, she nodded again, and stepped forward.

His hands on her upper arms were warm and reassuring as he helped her into the tub. There was a moment of awkwardness as she tried to lower herself into the water, but he held her firmly and lowered her safely into the warm suds, then eased her back so that she was lying in the water. She felt graceless and off balance with her hands behind her, but she was very aware of his hands, large and confident, on her. Hands she had known in both pleasure and pain, the kind of pain that melted into pleasure and made her ache for more. Just as she trusted those hands to bring her to pleasure after the pain, he was, silently, asking her to trust them to keep her safe, here, now, in the bath – but she was less trusting here, in this new environment, where she couldn't escape if she needed to.

He slid one hand under her back, and splashed warm water idly over her legs, belly and arms. She held herself stiffly, keenly aware of her own hands bound beneath her, of the weight of her body on her arms and wrists, holding them against the porcelain tub, but slowly, inexorably, the warm water and assurance in his hands did their job and she felt herself relaxing. She closed her eyes, giving herself over to his hands, to the familiarity of them on her skin, to the pleasure they always evoked in her. The tight knot she'd felt in her chest since he had tied her wrists loosened, and she sighed and sank deeper into the suds.

After a moment he lifted her to a sitting position and leant across her for the shampoo and poured some into the palm of one hand. She breathed in the familiar smell of his laundry soap and skin as she closed her eyes again and let her head drop back into his hand, compliant. A shudder ran through her as she felt his hands in her hair, tugging it up into a mass on the top of her head. He had pulled her hair before during sex, both sharply and gently, but every touch seemed magnified now, every cell in her body attuned to him in a way they never had been before.

She opened her eyes to find his gaze locked on hers, his mouth a breath away from hers. His breath tickled her mouth and his lips brushed hers in a fleeting touch before he pulled away. She let out a sigh of held breath, then allowed him to ease her back into the water until her hair floated all around her. Feeling the water close over her ears, her eyes drifted closed again, and she let herself float free, mindless; no fear, no anxiety. Even her hands in their bonds felt free.

His hand swirled her hair in the water, rinsing the shampoo out, and then she felt him begin to wash her, one hand still holding her up under her back, the other smoothing the soap over her skin in slow, languorous circles before sluicing water over to rinse her. The feel of his hand, slippery with soap and water, sliding over her skin made her breath come short; she drifted in a haze of sensuality and pleasure. And then his hand was on her breasts again, skimming over her skin and nipples tantalizingly before he went lower, moving down her torso to settle between her legs. Once there his fingers danced over the soft, pliant flesh, soapy fingers gliding across her cunt lips and clitoris in a way that was both pleasurable and frustrating. Over and over he stroked, but his touch was too light, his fingers too slick. She moaned, twisting towards him, but he held her still. Her eyes popped open and she glared up at him, panting. He only grinned down at her.

'Eric!' she said plaintively.

He put an innocent look on his face. 'What? Is there something you want? Something you need?'

She made a sound akin to a growl deep in her throat, sure that she would go mad with frustration, but swallowed it, recognising the game now, and realising that this game was by *his* rules, and there was nothing she could do about it.

He lifted her back to a sitting position. 'OK, waterbaby,' he said, 'time to get out of the bath.'

He helped her from the tub and cradled her against his body as he reached for a towel.

'I'm getting you wet!' she protested, leaning away from him, but he only pulled her tighter against his body, leaning back against the bathroom wall and holding her as she squirmed against him, armless, bound, helpless. She looked up at him, going suddenly still as she realised how helpless she really was. The fact that she couldn't pull away, or pull herself closer to him, that what he did with her was completely beyond her control, was made very real to her in that moment, and part of her resisted instinctively. She strained with renewed vigour to get closer to him, to feel every inch of herself against him. She arched against his body, pulling against the hold he had on her bound wrists, and buried her face in his neck, biting him softly.

'You little brat,' he said, chuckling as he pulled her away from him by the wrists and looked down at her. She panted, eyes locked on his, as he held her away from him. There was an intensity in his look that made her cunt throb anew, and she abruptly stopped squirming. Slowly, never taking his gaze from hers, he pulled her closer and began sliding her still wet body up and down his own. The coarse material of his jeans abraded her skin, inflaming her. The catch of his belt on her skin excited her. His shirt rubbed her bare nipples and she felt them harden against him, puckering like tiny, seeking mouths. He slid her down onto a knee that he pushed between her thighs, balancing her there, holding her still when she would have ground herself against him.

She moaned and closed her eyes, surrendering at last to the feel of his hands on her, the calluses on the tips of his fingers softened by the slip of the water as he ran his hands up and down the wet length of her body. Unable to help herself, she pressed harder against him, then stilled as his hands curled around the rope that bound her wrists.

'Oh no,' he said. 'Not yet.'

She raised her face to his and stared at him, transfixed, every part of her awareness there, in the palms of his hands, holding her, binding her. Keeping one hand on her wrists, he brought the other to the nape of her neck and pulled her roughly to him. Covering her mouth with his, he kissed her deeply, then pulled away and looked down into her eyes. She felt that she was only tethered to the earth by the hands that held her to him, one at the nape of her neck, one on her bound wrists.

'I've wanted you like this for so long,' he said, his voice hoarse. Never loosening her wrists, he kissed her eyes, her cheeks, her throat. He dipped his head farther and took first one taut, wet nipple and then the other into his mouth. She writhed against him, struggling against his hold on her and the rope's bite on her wrists, but not in fear this time. His grip tightened and he lowered her back to the floor, pushing her thighs apart with one hand while he held her wrists tightly with the other, bending her back by them, forcing her to open herself to him. She gasped as he sank his face between her legs, lapping at the moisture he found there, then ran his mouth in a trail up her body to her lips. She tasted herself on his tongue and gasped again as he bit her neck. She felt the bulge in his jeans and pressed against it, delirious with heat and desire, but, chuckling again, he drew back from her, denying her what she wanted so desperately. Hovering over her, not allowing her contact with him, he used her wrists as a handle and bent her further back, then just held her there, while he ran his other hand over her body almost negligently.

Keeping his eyes on her face, he laid his hand against the mound of her pubis. She whimpered and pushed against his palm, but he held her still by the ropes on her wrists. He slid his fingers along her cunt lips, stroking, teasing, all the while watching the expressions move across her face.

'Please,' she finally gasped, opening her legs to him. 'Please?'

With almost painful deliberation he edged one finger just inside her, and then, as she opened herself more fully to him, another. He leant over her and brought his mouth close to hers.

'Please what?' he asked, still teasing her with his fingers, still denying her the feel of his body against hers.

She took a shuddering breath. 'Please – I want your fingers inside me,' she finally said.

He smiled at her, sweetly, and then pushed his fingers deep inside her.

She cried out as he did and bucked against him, straining upwards against the rope, devouring his fingers with her cunt. Seesawing her between his hands, one on her wrists, the other in her cunt, he pushed her, thrusting his fingers in and out while he pressed down on her clit with his thumb, driving her to the edge of orgasm.

She twisted and moaned, sure that he would deny her again, desperate for the release she had been denied over and over.

But then she was there, and he wasn't stopping, he was saying, 'Yes, yes, yes,' over and over and she was coming, shattering, the only thing holding her together the rope on her wrists. Her body shook with the force of it and he let her wrists go to scoop an arm around her as she sank back to the floor.

Cradling her against him, he lifted her up and carried her to the couch. As her breathing slowed, he lay down next to her, pulling her body against his, and worked the wet knots loose. As her hands came free she cried out softly – not from pain, but from a strange feeling of loss. She brought her hands around in front of her and rubbed the marks on her wrists, staring at them in wonder. She looked over at him as though seeing him for the first time.

'Thank you,' she said.

He raised her wrists to his mouth, kissing each one where the ropes had left their mark. 'Thank *you*,' he said, 'for trusting me.'

I Am
by Tamsin Flowers

I am a dominatrix. Yes, I thought your eyes would light up when you heard me say that. My name is Belladonna and tonight you will be my slave. You will obey my every command and, if you don't, you will feel the pain of my anger and the sting of my hand. Do you understand?

Of course you do.

I am a dominatrix and I am in command. Now you may come into my room. Stand here in the light so I can get a good look at you. I must judge whether you have the potential to satisfy me; my standards are high and I doubt whether you will be able to quench the fires that burn within me. Your looks are nothing remarkable. Your face won't sear itself into my memory and torment my sleep in the way that my face will torment yours. That's right – take a good look at my features because you will never want to forget them by the time I've finished with you.

Look at my long black hair, so shiny, falling nearly to my waist in a raven twist of tumbling curls caught up in a blood-red ribbon. Look upon my porcelain white skin, nearly translucent, so soft and perfectly unmarked apart from the dark beauty spot by my mouth. And then you discover the soft curve of my lips, dark red and wine-stained. I am smiling at you now; you will come to fear these lips when they sneer at you in anger. But the feature that will captivate you the most is my eyes. Look hard into their pools of emerald green. Deep and unknowable and swimming with secrets. Sometimes they flash with anger or sparkle with laughter; sometimes they are swirling with mysteries that you can know nothing about. They will drive you wild and you will be haunted by them for the rest of your life.

I can see that just looking at me makes your breath quicken. I am slim and strong and my corset is tightly laced so it leaves nothing to the imagination. But I keep most of my charms hidden under this black velvet cape so I can tease and tantalise you. You will only be allowed to see what I want you to see even though you are desperate to see all of me. I doubt whether that will be possible. I can hardly be expected to reveal myself to a man like you. But you can see how long and shapely my legs are. And look at the arch of my foot, encased in soft red leather stilettos with the sharpest and highest of heels. If you do not behave yourself, you might feel exactly how sharp those heels are, if I think it necessary to keep you under control. Do not tempt me by disobeying my orders. You will very quickly come to regret it if you do not do exactly as you are told.

I am a dominatrix and I am in total control. The man who brought you to me told me that you had been bad and that you needed to be punished. That you wanted to be punished. Look around my room and I think you'll agree that you have come to the right place. See, over there, my collection of whips hanging on the wall. Which one would you like to feel across your buttocks? The long black bullwhip with the elegant braided handle? My short suede flogger with more than 30 tails? Or perhaps the gold-studded paddle? Imagine the marks that will make on your yielding white flesh. But I will choose which one I use on you. The choice will not be yours because you are here to be punished, not to enjoy. See my rack of crops and canes. Can you imagine the sound they will make as they slice through the air towards your flesh? The pain I will be able to inflict as first you beg for more and then you beg me to stop.

172

But you will be powerless. I have plenty of ways of restraining you and I can tell that you need to be restrained already. You have seen what lies in store for you and you can hardly control your excitement, can you? But you must or I will not be able to work with you.

So, it is time to begin. Do exactly as I say or you will feel my anger rather than my playful side. Do you understand? Good. Now take off your clothes. All of them. Don't hesitate, for you can hide nothing from me. I deal with men like you every day – you're nothing special to look at. The only way you can awaken my interest is by obeying my commands. Come here so I can put you into position for what I have planned.

These are the cuffs that I am going to attach to your wrists. They are lined in red velvet and you might think that would make them soft. But you will find that when you strain against them, the hard steel underneath the velvet will press into your flesh and bite into your wrists. Their purpose is to control you, not to cosset you. Give me your right hand. There, wasn't that a satisfying click as the cuff closed around your wrist? I can see by the way you are biting your lip that this is just what you need. Now, I will have your left hand, that's a good boy. Another small click and you are truly in my power.

The two cuffs are joined by a length of strong chain. Step over here and raise your arms above your head. Watch me as I climb onto this chair in front of you; it brings my mound close to your face. If you breathe in deeply you might smell my musky perfume. But that isn't why I've climbed up here. No, from here I am able to clip the chain from your wrists onto this strong steel ring on my ceiling. Now I have you chained up, ready for my pleasure. Soon the blood will have left your arms, your muscles will burn and your wrists will be in agony. But why should I care? It is all part of your punishment and you came here to be punished, didn't you?

So, you think you can lean forward to bring your face

even closer to my most private and secret area. How dare you! Did that hurt? That was my favourite crop. I like to use it across the back of your knees, a small punishment for your little misdemeanour and a gentle taste of the pain that awaits you. I heard your sharp little intake of breath and I know that was what you wanted to feel, what you'd been waiting all day to feel. Well, we have hardly begun. But because you were so naughty, I have another punishment to inflict upon you. Yes, now I am blindfolding you with this dark, heavy blindfold. You do not deserve to watch me go about my work. You have lost that privilege and now you must prove to me that you can be good before I will let you look at me again. You will not be able to see what I am about to do to you; you will only feel the pain as I inflict it upon you. And I will be doing that without mercy until you beg me to stop. Then, perhaps, I will let you see what you may never touch.

As you are restrained and blindfolded, I can take my time to look at you and I will use the sharp tip of my bamboo cane to trace the shape of your muscles and to test the firmness of your body. I like the way you writhe under its touch as I trace the fine long curve of your back and let the tip of the cane rest on the rising curve of your buttock. You are longing to feel its sting, aren't you? But first I must finish my inspection.

With a push of my satin-gloved hand I can twist you round on your chain, your bare feet stumbling on the floor as your tired arms are forced to bear your weight. You have a broad, strong chest, narrowing down to a tense rigid six pack. Small curls of dark hair lead my eyes downwards and I trace the path with the tip of my bamboo. Down to your impressive manhood, though I won't say that aloud for you to hear. It is half erect, but as I run the point along the shaft it bucks to life and surges upwards, straight and hard. You are ready for me now. You want my ministrations and I know that you will like them very much.

With a quick jab, I spin you round again and there, with a

swish and a slap – you feel it, for the first time, the sting of my small cane across your buttocks. You grunt and your breathing quickens. I watch you brace your legs, ready for more, and I watch as a sharp red line appears across each of your creamy white cheeks. I don't want your legs braced so in one swift move I kick them out from under you and administer another smack, this time slightly lower. You let out a small yelp but I can see that a vein in your cock is pulsating as you become more and more turned on by what is happening to you. I strike you again and again. It is my job to see that the pain outweighs the pleasure. After all, you are here to be punished. You have admitted that much yourself.

A criss-cross pattern of red welts spreads across your buttocks and the backs of your thighs. You are slumped in the handcuffs. It did not take you long to learn not to brace your legs – the sting of my bamboo saw to that. You are groaning as you wait for the next blow but your cock is as hard as ever. I am moving quietly around the room. I take my work seriously and I can feel that I have broken out in a sweat. I have been putting all my strength into your beating and your cries tell me that you appreciate my handiwork. I let my velvet cape slip to the floor. Now I am starting to feel turned on too and I let my hand slide between my legs for a quick caress.

It's time for a change of pace. I swap my cane for the gold-studded paddle, slamming it hard against you in a flurry of rapid slaps. You let out a succession of sharp, high cries and now I feel that I am beginning to get somewhere with you. Standing in front of you, I gently stroke your cheek and you turn to my hand to try and kiss it. That is not allowed and again you feel the harsh bite of my golden paddle. Your hips thrust backwards to meet each slap and your breathing has become frenzied. I stop and wait while you beg for more. I like to hear you pleading so I rest for a while.

As your whimpering subsides, I slip out of my corset. I look down at my round, swollen breasts, so soft and smooth. My nipples are pierced with silver rings and I pull on them gently, making myself groan. Your cock bucks in response to the sound and I remember I have work to do. I walk slowly towards you and I can tell that you are straining to hear my breathing. As I come right up close you can feel the heat of my body and I can feel yours. You press your hips forwards against me, so I slap you with my hand. 'Please ...' you whisper – but I must punish you some more.

I pull the blindfold off your eyes and you gasp as you take in my naked body. It is very beautiful with soft curves and pure white skin. There is no hair between my legs and I watch you greedily eyeing my fanny that glistens with the wetness gently seeping from within. I glance down. The pink rosebud of my clit is protruding, waiting to be touched and so I brush my hand gently against it. You groan and twitch. I know you want me but you cannot have me. You have not yet earned that privilege; perhaps you never will.

I walk to the far corner of the room, to where I keep my box of tricks. With my legs apart, I bend down from the waist to find what I am after and I know that you are enjoying the view. Can you see how wet my pussy is? It looks so inviting that I can hear you pulling against you chains as my juices run down the insides of my thighs. I root through the box and, at last, I find it. As I turn and come to the centre of the room, I strap on a giant red dildo. Slowly, as I tighten the straps, the hard rubber cock stands out proud from the front of my cunt. It is far larger than your cock and it gives me a feeling of power. I stand straight and tall in front of you, holding the shaft in my right hand, laughing at the fear that has crept into your eyes.

Yes, this is part of your punishment too. You thought you would get to fuck me. But it is I who is going to do the fucking today. I am going to take you and make you mine. As I walk around behind you, you start to whimper again.

But there is no going back now – I will have my satisfaction.

Your buttocks are red and raw from the beating but I have a special salve that will help them to heal. I unscrew the pot and take a handful of the musky gloop. I spread it gently across your backside and you slump and groan as you appreciate the slick, cold greasiness of it. Then I let my fingers slide between your cheeks, gently spreading the lubricant as I kick your legs apart with my feet. Your muscles tighten as I push my fingers inside you, but this is nothing compared with what is about to come. I spread more of the salve on my huge false cock and then I run the tip of it up and down your crack. You strain away from me but you cannot go far, and I know deep down you don't want to – otherwise you wouldn't be here. I rub harder and faster; you groan as your muscles start to relax under my continued pressure. Slowly I push the hard red plastic into you and then draw it back out. Then in again and out. I pick up speed and you cry out. It hurts in the best possible way, doesn't it? I know because I am an expert at this. I have done it many times so I know exactly when to slow down and when to pull back and then when to surge hard forward.

As I fuck you harder and harder, I wrap my arms around your front and my hands find your cock, throbbing and pulsing with my every thrust. I grip it tightly and you shout and arch your back. You are about to come but I cannot let you, so I pull sharply out of you from behind and step back. Your hips are jerking backwards and forwards as you desperately try to make contact with me again and I laugh at your frustration.

'Beg for it,' I whisper as I reach for my favourite crop. 'You've been a bad boy and you have to beg.' And, as I beat you with the crop, you beg for me again and again. Now you are my slave. I pull the chair over and climb up to undo your chain. You drop to the floor but I have not let you down so you can rest. I unstrap the dildo and toss it to one side. Then I sit on the chair with my legs wide apart. It is your turn to pleasure me. I will not finish your punishment until I have been fully satisfied.

On your hands and knees in front of me I tell you to come closer. Then I reach for your head and push it deeply between my legs. My clitoris is throbbing – you must suck it hard to give me the deepest of orgasms. I feel your lips and your teeth and your tongue envelop it, unleashing a torrent of sensation through my body, making me arch my back. I still have my crop; if you let up in your efforts for just one moment I give you a sharp sting across your back. But you understand what you have to do and you work hard, sucking deeply and twisting your tongue around and around my swollen bud. Finally, with a surge of pleasure that makes me feel as if I was being turned inside out, I climax. But I do not let you stop. Even as I shudder on the chair I beat you harder and then I climax again and again.

Exhausted you slump to the floor but I haven't finished with you. As I gently trail the tails of my flogger across your back your cock springs to life once more. I know it won't take much to finish the job but I tease you with the whip until, again, you are begging. I bend you over the chair and administer the coup de grâce. The 30 tails leave fresh marks across your back and legs as you writhe under its magic touch. Finally, with a roar, you find release and, as you arch upward, the chair tumbles over. You are sprawled at my feet, bucking and grunting as a spurt of white semen falls hot across my ankles. You stare up at me with gratitude and wonder in your eyes.

I am a dominatrix. And I aim to please.

You are my slave and your punishment has been successful.

Slam Me Down
by Thomas Fuchs

OK, here's the problem. For me, there's nothing like a good fuck. I mean getting it right up the ass. And what I really like is doing it with someone for the first time. It's kind of like trying out a new restaurant or something. Except you probably haven't read any reviews. There's a kind of build-up, wondering, how good will he be? How's his technique? Good finger work to start? Will he move them in fast or slow, does he know how to work them back and forth, how to stroke my prostate, make that little gland hum with happiness? And then when he pulls his fingers out, there's that delicious moment, like waiting for the main course, and then he's pushing his dick in. If I'm a little tight, will he stay hard? How much pain will there be, how long will it last before it becomes such sweet pleasure? Will he just be a slugger or will he be a dancer? Will we get a hot rhythm going? Has he got the stamina and the control to go and go and go until that magic final moment? You know what I mean.

So what's the problem? For me, it's three little words. No, not the ones you're thinking of. The ones I mean are "wrestle for top". Have you ever heard that phrase? Well, that's the problem. I love to wrestle and I'm very good, but as I've explained, I really like being topped by a hot guy. A lot of guys think if you dominate them on the mat you should fuck them. You can dominate and still be the one fucked, you know!

I'm 5'9", 175, solid through and through. Big chest and arms, great legs. Cute butt. And I'm pretty well hung – 7.5", cut, with nice balls, or so I've been told. I'm 24 years old. Took judo when I was a kid, wrestled in high school. Didn't wrestle in college. Didn't have time for the training. But I've stayed in shape and I like to wrestle. I like the contact, and like the game, outmanoeuvring the other guy, beating him down, making him submit. I get hard all right and I could fuck the guy if I had to, and I'm versatile and I like to fuck, but as I say, for me, nothing beats that thrill when a guy's about to top you for the first time.

So, I'll give you a typical case. This happened not too long ago. I respond to a guy on Craigslist who says he wants to wrestle. We swap stats and pics, and I like what I see, if he's telling the truth and using a real photo. His name is Kurt. Of course, I don't know if that's his real name, but it's nice and butch, don't you think? My name's Donny, by the way. We swap a little chat, and we both want to do it in the nude, no wrestling gear or briefs or anything. Then he asks me, 'Wrestle for top?'

I reply, 'Winner's choice.'

'OK,' he says.

I hope he's a good fucker, but of course that's not something you can tell by emailing a guy or even talking to him. It's time to meet.

So Saturday morning I go over to his place. He opens the door and, right away, things are looking good. Just like the specs and his pic: six feet, 185 pounds or so, a little chest hair, hairy legs, very nicely outfitted with what looked to be a good eight inches, pretty thick, but not so big that he's gonna wreck me.

He's got his place pretty well set up for wrestling. Some guys want to do it on the bed or maybe put a couple of mattresses on the floor, but he's got regulation mats laid out. He seems to be a no-bullshit guy. I'm not worried that he's three inches taller and ten pounds heavier than me. Just makes the wrestling challenge all the more interesting. I really like a good hard match.

We circle each other on the mat. I make a move on him, trying to grab an arm to set him up for a throw or a lock but he slips out of range – he's fast – and then he launches his own attack. I'll spare you all the details but pretty quick he's got me in a classic abdominal stretch. If you like to watch hot wrestlers, you know this move and you love it. Bend the victim back while he's still on his feet, really stretching him out. Hurts him like hell and really shows off his abs, if he's got the cuts, which of course I do.

'Like this move, little guy?' he says. He's trying to taunt me. That's part of the game, you know, talking rough and all that. I look down at my ripped abs and I tell him I'm looking so hot, it makes me want to suck myself.

He puts on more pressure. 'Give, pussy boy?'

Hmmm, I think to myself, *pussy boy* – this is promising.' I know I should just give up and beg for mercy. 'Let me go, big guy. Please, please let me go. You're soooo tough.' That would get him nice and hard and get me what I want. But I have my pride and I don't want to give. I guess I'm just a very butch bottom.

I know a counter to the ab stretcher and I do it; it's hard to explain, involves bending your legs, which goes against your natural instincts, but it can throw your opponent off balance if he's not ready for it, which this guy wasn't. I get out of the hold, get under his arm and flip him onto the mat. He lands flat and hard. A real slam, but he's got fight left in him and he starts to sit up.

I jump behind him, get my legs around his sides and squeeze the hell out of him. He's thrashing around trying to get out, tries pulling at my legs, but my legs are really strong and I'm crushing the life out of him. His face is getting red and his arms are starting to just sort of flop around without pulling at me very hard.

I reach down and give him a little slap on the face. 'What's the matter, stud,' I say. 'You in over your head?'

'Fuck you,' he says. But he has trouble saying it, like he's gasping. I give him an extra hard squeeze with my legs.

'Give!'

'Fuck you,' he says. And there's the problem. How's he going to be able to fuck me if I have to squeeze the life out of him? I'm thinking I really better get him to submit before he's all worn out and nothing more than a hunk of knocked-out meat.

I keep my legs wrapped around him, but I go for that pain point just at the base of the nose. I press it really hard and he lets out one hell of a yowl. Turns out he's got a pretty low pain threshold.

'Shit, man, that's cheating,' he says.

'Give?'

'Fuck you.'

'Hope so,' I say. I'm laughing.

He doesn't answer, just tries to break free. So I give him the nose point again and, at the same time, grab a really good point under the ear and squeeze that and it must feel like he's got lightning or a steel bolt going through his head. Imagine the worst headache you've ever had. He's writhing around and screaming. A lot.

'I give, I give, I give.' It pours out of him. I let go and he flops back down on the mat.

'OK,' he says, 'you won.' Then after a little bit, he says, 'Lube and stuff over there,' pointing to a cabinet.

'You don't want to go two out of three?' I ask, and smile.

'Don't rub it in, bud. You won. You get to top me. Fuck me good, OK?'

So then this thought occurs to me. 'Wait a minute,' I say. 'You didn't throw this fight, did you?'

'What?'

'Let me win, so I'd fuck you?'

'Naw. You won, dude. This time.' Then, finally, it dawns

on this guy; maybe he's a little slow. 'You want me to fuck you,' he says.

'You like my ass?' I turn and show it off to him. I am pretty hot in that department. Well-muscled ass. I can do great things with it. Want to do great things with this boy if I can get him up and going again after the beat down I've given him.

'Yeah, man,' he says. 'I'll do you. Do you good.' That's what he says, but he's still just lying there. I straddle him, sitting low on his stomach, his cock just behind me. I slap him, pretty hard. I figure if I can piss him off, that'll give him his strength back.

'Hey, dude. Don't do that,' he says.

'You gonna stop me? You gonna show me what a man you are?'

Then I lean down and lick a nipple. He begins breathing deep. I suck it a little, tongue it some more. It's hard now. I switch over to the other one, give it the same treatment. I feel his dick moving behind me, and when I look over my shoulder, I see it's showing a little life, starting to stiffen up, but there's a way to go yet. Damn it, I won the match but I still have to work away on this guy to get what I want – what I deserve, damn it!

So now I'm down stroking the top of his inner leg, doing a stimulation thing, and after a little bit of this, I can see that it's having a good result. The veins on his dick are swelling, and the whole thing is getting bigger and rising up a little. The snake is finally waking up!

His balls are hairy, so I don't really want to use my tongue on them. Instead, I use my famous "claw technique". It's not really a claw, of course. I get my fingers up under and behind his nuts, just slightly curled up against the back and wiggle my fingers a little as I bring my hand up around to the front. This works great. His dick pops up, falling back almost to his abs.

So I raise myself back up and get my tongue going on the

head of his dick. Give a few quick flicks and then a nice long lick from the bottom of the shaft up to the top of the head. A couple of drops of precome ooze out. I flick that away with my finger and then I go down him. I'm a pretty good cocksucker. I take him all the way in, to the back of my mouth, and then I slide back, keeping it hot and wet for him all the way, using my tongue for extra effect.

'Oh, God,' he says. 'That's so good.'

Now, I'm doing a real vacuum job on him, sucking and sliding up and down. Makes the inside of my mouth tingle just right. Because of the way that I'm wired, I guess, this sets my ass to twitching, like an itch that needs to be scratched on the inside. I want this cock in me! But after all my work, he's still just lying there. Is this wrestler stud going to turn out to be a dud? You'd think he'd be all over me by now. I guess I'm making it too easy for him. He's having too good a time just lying there.

I stop blowing him and open up one of the condoms, slide it on him and lube it good. Then I work some around and up into my hole. Give my finger a little squeeze with my butt. Man, I've got such great control! I can make a top so happy.

I get back on him, lower myself onto his dick. Ahhh ... good, it's staying hard. I do a couple of squats, not going all the way down, taking just the head into me, teasing it and giving me a chance to open up a little. He's taking slow, deep breaths. That's good. That'll help him keep hard. Now I slide all the way down, taking him deep inside me, feeling it push past my pleasure gland and in deep. Ummmm ... Yummy ... feels nice. He's going 'Ah, ah' and someone's got these growls coming from deep in their throat. Oh, wait, that's me!

He's making the shivery energy shoot all through me! But still, I'm doing most of the work. Is this fair, I ask you? My thighs are beginning to ache from doing these squats. I'm in great shape, but remember I had to crush him good

184

when we were wrestling so now I've got to have a break, don't I? I give him a couple more squeezes. He likes that, starts bucking his hips. I'm a bad boy, I guess, 'cause I slap my dick against his face a couple of times.

'Don't do that, partner,' he says, so I slide off him and get on my knees, which is one of my favourite ways to get it, with my butt up high.

He's got all his strength back by now so he's on me, and pretty quick he's got his cock back in me, and I have to say he does have a fine technique – deep and slow and, when he's all the way in, I give him a squeeze and then I let him go and he slides back and then in again. Turns out he's really a pretty nice guy. He's making it as good as he can for me – reaching around, getting hold of my dick and pumping me at the same pace he's fucking me. The good, good feeling is surging all through me, up my ass and all along my cock. I gotta say he was doing a fine job on me, made me light up all over. At some point he lets go of me and I start pumping myself. I'm just gonna come and then he pulls out and gives this big kind of shout, a groan, and then I feel the heavy hot slap of his come landing on my back. Once, twice, a couple more times. He's shooting all over me.

Finally, I rear back and let go across the mat. Great huge gobs of it. Even I'm impressed.

A little bit later, he's saying how hot the whole thing was and that we should do it again – how he wants another chance to wrestle me down. I'm polite and say, 'Sure, stud' and stuff like that, but I don't know. I guess what I'm looking for is a guy who can wrestle me down for sure and then fuck me without me having to revive him or anything. I'm looking for a real man to wrestle. Is that so much to ask? Any takers? Any of you guys think you're man enough? Please?

The Constantly Horny Gardener
by Kyoko Church

Shirley pulled off her gardening gloves, swept an errant lock of blonde hair off her forehead, sat back on her heels in the dirt and sighed. Surveying the tiny shoots of green protruding from the black earth, she smiled vaguely. *Now I understand why people find gardening so relaxing*, she thought. It was nice out in the warm summer sun seeing the fruits of one's labour starting to manifest into something tangible. Yes, gardening, she thought. That's the perfect hobby for me.

Back inside her home Shirley poured a glass of water and sat down in front of her laptop. With dinner already prepared she had about an hour before the kids would be home from school, before her quiet sanctuary would be transformed into the bustling hub of activity it always became, when snacks and drinks and help with homework would be demanded and her duty as referee between her two pre-teen boys would be required. Not long after that Marcus would be home from work and it would be the mad rush to get dinner on the table and eat before chauffeuring her sons to their various after-school activities.

I'm so lucky, Shirley reminded herself, so lucky to have this idyllic life. And if, recently, she'd found herself a little bored, perhaps a little restless, it was certainly just because her boys were growing up, becoming more independent. She just needed to find herself a hobby, something to interest her and fill her time, especially with summer holidays starting next week and the boys off at camp. And what better hobby for her than gardening?

Firing up the internet, she did a Google search on her new pastime. For the next 20 minutes she clicked absently through various pages, all manner of plants, flowers and foliage flipping past her eyes. The scope of it daunted her and she began to feel uneasy about the little vegetable patch Marcus had dug out for her in the backyard. In the end she found herself in a gardening chatroom.

Posted by: NewbieGardener
I am new to gardening and just planted a small veggie patch. Any advice?

For the next five minutes Shirley stared expectantly at the thread she'd started. There was no response. Feeling foolish, she was just about to close the window when suddenly text appeared below hers.

Posted by: Master G
What've u planted?

She wrote back quickly.

Posted by: NewbieGardener
Just green beans, cucumbers and carrots for now.

Master G responded, offering his encouragement. As their thread lengthened, Shirley relaxed and began to enjoy their chat. Master G seemed very knowledgeable and patient with what she imagined were her basic questions. She thanked him saying she imagined the G must be for Gardener, since he certainly seemed to be a master at that.

```
Posted by: Master G
No, not for gardening, for Geoffrey. But
I am a master.
```

Huh? She hesitated, not knowing how to respond.

```
Posted by: Master G
What's ur name, since we're getting
acquainted?
```

She hesitated again. Certainly giving your real name to some stranger on the internet was not a good idea. Not to mention that her name always made people think she was 30 years older than she actually was. Damn family name. How many 30-something Shirleys were there? Well, what did she care anyway? It was only her first name.

```
Posted by: NewbieGardener
I'm Shirley.
```

```
Posted by: Master G
Fine then, don't tell me ;)
```

Shirley giggled. She spent the next few minutes trying to convince him that Shirley was indeed her real name, even though she wasn't 60.

```
Posted by: NewbieGardener
My name does suit me. I am just the
stay-at-home mum of two boys. May as
well call me June Cleaver.
```

She hit Enter and then felt foolish again. Why was she telling him this? She glanced at the clock. The boys would be home soon. She should get going. She told Master G.

What? Was he being ...? Just then the front door opened and she heard her boys come bustling in. Her heart beating in her chest, she quickly shut down the chatroom window.

'Hey, Mum! We're starving!' they shouted. Shirley, her cheeks flushed, brought the top of her laptop down shut for good measure. Patting the sides of her hair she stood up.

'In here, boys,' she replied. 'I'll make you a snack.'

One of the many things Shirley appreciated about her husband was his predictability. Marcus rose every morning at 7 a.m. and left for work promptly at 7.45 a.m. For his lunch that Shirley packed for him, he liked a ham and cheese sandwich with four pickled onions, a small carton of milk and an apple. On Fridays he also enjoyed an oatmeal cookie and the milk was chocolate. He arrived home every evening at 5.30 p.m. Sunday nights they had dinner with his parents. Wednesday nights he played tennis with a friend. Shirley never had to wonder where he was or when he would call. She never had to guess at what might please him or what their plans would be.

This being nearly 9.30 p.m. on Friday night, she knew what that meant too. Shirley dressed for bed and stood in front of the mirror, brushing her hair and thinking about what would happen next. Marcus would reach under her tanktop and fondle her breasts for approximately five minutes before he moved his hand lower, inside her panties, readying her with his fingers for another five. Then he would strip off her panties and his boxers and lower himself on top of her. Marcus was so gentle and caring in their lovemaking, she thought happily. He knew exactly when to push her legs together under his and press his pelvis firmly against hers to bring her to her climax. He always waited for that and not every man would, she thought. Then, two minutes later, he would finish and would be soundly snoring beside her by 9.45 p.m.

Shirley wasn't exactly sure why, but tonight after she slipped into bed and he began his usual foreplay routine, she got a notion in her head. As Marcus's fingers gently tugged at her nipples she began to think about that Christmas party two years ago. Her husband never drank more than two beers or perhaps a glass of wine if they were having dinner with friends. But this night Marcus's new boss poured him a mixed drink and Marcus, not wanting to disappoint or offend the man, drank it. After the third one Shirley's usually buttoned-up, straight-laced husband was telling jokes, laughing and clapping his boss on the back. When one joke got a little racy, she realised she'd better take him home.

In bed that night, even though it was a Saturday, Marcus had reached for her in a way that he never had before, a way that had more force and was almost ... brutal. He put his hand on top of her head and pushed it, firmly, toward his groin. There was no question what he wanted. When she took him in her mouth, the groan that escaped his throat was unlike any sound he usually made, guttural and base. Holding the back of her head by her blonde hair he thrust and thrust into her mouth, sometimes so deeply it made her gag and gasp for air. He came in her mouth, hard and without warning, or so it seemed to Shirley, as she choked down his come, eyes watering. As Marcus lay snoring beside her that cold December night two years ago, Shirley lay awake, marvelling at what had just happened, trying to make sense of it. And of the wetness and wanting it left between her legs.

Now, on their usual night and with things proceeding on target, the memory seemed incongruous, like something that happened to somebody else. But it was them. With the

191

sound of that groan he'd made echoing in her head, Shirley did then what she never did. Gently pushing her husband's hand away she moved down to settle between his legs.

'Sweetheart, what are you doing?' Marcus asked. His shaft was already erect and she took it in her hand. But when she lowered her head to him he stopped her. 'Darling, please,' he said softly, pulling her back up to him.

'I just thought we could do something a little, I don't know, different tonight,' Shirley whispered as he held her and stroked her hair.

'My angel, that's no place for a man's wife to put her mouth.' He held her, gazing into her eyes. 'Why would you do that?'

'Well, it's just,' Shirley took a breath. 'Remember that night a couple of years back? I think it was after that Christmas party. And you had me go down ...'

'Shhh, no, don't talk about it.' Marcus said, looking away. 'I'm sorry for that. It was terrible of me. I never should have treated you that way–'

'No, it's OK. If you want that, if you want me to ...' Shirley stammered. But Marcus wouldn't hear it.

'Darling, no. You don't have to do anything so base. You are my beautiful wife. I love you and I love our lovemaking. I don't want anything else.' He kissed her gently then, pulling her body close.

Yes, Marcus was a thoughtful and gentle lover. Attentive to her needs and so respectful to her as a woman. Shirley was certainly very lucky. And after they had made love that night, Marcus bringing her to orgasm and then finishing inside her as usual, Shirley lay beside her sleeping husband and a thought occurred to her. Why did she keep reminding herself how lucky she was? Who was she trying to convince?

Outside in her garden that summer, Shirley pulled little weeds from around her cucumbers and giggled quietly to herself. Master G had told her a funny joke about cucumbers yesterday, what was it now? Something about an old man flashing his tomatoes to make them red, and when the old lady tried it there was no change in the tomatoes but ... She giggled again. 'The cucumbers are huge!' she said aloud to herself, laughing.

It had been about a month since that first exchange and what Shirley now realised was just her being silly and prudish about Master G's bawdy sense of humour. With the boys away at camp, she'd been lonely. Plus she'd needed help with her fledgling attempts at gardening; really, that's why she'd gone back in the gardening chatroom. They'd chatted again there then moved to instant messaging which was much faster and not limited to gardening talk, since they often went off on tangents about everything from music to literature to news headlines. His humour could get a little risqué at times, and Shirley wasn't the kind of woman who usually went in for off-coloured remarks. But something about Master G's sly wit made her relish a little naughtiness.

Shirley glanced at her watch and began gathering together her gardening implements. Recently she and Master G had fallen into the habit of messaging every morning around 10 a.m. and that time was fast approaching. She smiled to herself as she thought, not for the first time, how she looked forward to their chats. And the only reason she hadn't mentioned her new friend to Marcus was because she didn't think Marcus would appreciate the naughty remarks. Marcus, for as much as she loved him, could be a little bit of a prude at times.

It was silly, she thought, how she continued to think of him as "Master G". She'd called him Geoffrey once, early on in their chatting, but he'd insisted on his IM tag.

Shirley sat down at her laptop and logged in at ten on the dot. Her tag was "SexyShirley36", as a little joke between them from the first time they chatted. Master G was there and they talked for a while before she told him she felt silly still calling him "Master G"– that couldn't she call him Geoffrey?

Master G: U know what to call me.

She smiled. Sometimes he liked to make jokes like this, tease her. Acting all serious and commanding. Like he was her boss, or something. Well, fine, she would play along this time.

SexyShirley36: Oh yes, Master G, sir. What else could I do for you, oh exalted one?

Master G: Well this is a welcum change. There is something u can do for me. Tell me something.

SexyShirley36: Yes, anything for you, sir.

Master G: How often do u masturbate?

Shirley gasped. Heat rushed to her cheeks and she sat frozen in her chair, wanting to shut down the window, knowing she should end this, but somehow not being able to do anything. After a minute:

Master G: Cum now, Sexy S. There are certain details I need to know.

SexyShirley36: What? I don't know what you're talking about. Are you still teasing me?

Master G: Well, not yet, but I hope to

start soon.

Shirley swallowed hard. This time she did shut her laptop. Not slamming it shut, but just slowly closing down her program and lowering the screen. She sat there staring at it. Her cheeks were still flushed and her heart beat fast.

Shirley couldn't pinpoint the moment when her life turned upside down. She didn't know the exact word or phrase from Master G that was the cause of her undoing. All she knew was that the life she was embroiled in now was so much blurrier than the black and white world she'd been used to. So much darker and sordid. Nasty and twisted.

And so much more exciting.

Master G was in charge now. He was clear: solemnly vow to follow my instruction. If you fail a task you must immediately confess to me. There will be punishments. But you will get what you so badly need.

It began with the masturbation issue.

Shirley swore she never masturbated. She could barely type the word. The thought of touching herself, well, it just seemed obscene. But Master G had pressed her: Really, you've never even rubbed against something? Humped a table corner? Pressed a little long against the spinning washing machine? Well, then it came out about the vacuum cleaner.

Shirley kept her house as neat as a pin. And the little treat at the end of vacuuming started innocently enough. She'd pulled the handle back at the wrong angle and bumped the end of it softly against her crotch. Oh, the vibrations! They went right through her, to her core it seemed. She remembered it was a Friday afternoon, a week since her husband had last touched her so her flesh was primed with longing. As she continued to press against the buzzing handle it didn't take long before the vibrations sent her over the edge and she'd doubled over it, panting with relief. She

195

barely acknowledged to herself what she was doing. But that's when she started vacuuming three times a week.

Master G found this out and all of Shirley's intimate secrets she would never share with anyone else. He knew about her "schedule" with Marcus. He knew about that Christmas when Marcus had forced himself into her mouth, and how he wouldn't let it happen again, even though she'd offered. He knew that it secretly excited her. And, Shirley had begun to think, he even knew things about her, about what she wanted, what she *needed,* that she didn't know herself.

Take the email that she'd opened up one morning, shortly after admitting her use of the vacuum cleaner, for example.

From: Master G
To: SexyShirley36

So your husband fucking you once a week isn't enough? You need to get yourself off another three times a week with electrically powered household appliances? Do you need to cum that badly? My, you really are a horny little slut, aren't you? Somebody needs to take you in hand, slut. Somebody needs to teach you that you only exist to please men, as a fuck tool for your husband and a receptacle for his seed. Somebody needs to take control of that horny, wet, cum-crazy little pussy. And that somebody is me. From now on, you may cum only when I say you may. Any unsanctioned orgasms will be punished with further denial. And I expect total honesty. For now, as a reward for your candour of late, you may continue to pleasure yourself with the vacuum, but you may not cum. Under no circumstances will you allow yourself to orgasm. You will await my further instructions.

Shirley read this email again and again. Her eyes were wide, glazed and she realised after the fourth or fifth read that she'd had her fist pressed into her mouth. The things he called her! The filthy language. It was totally obscene. And yet her heart beating was only matched by the pulse between her thighs.

She'd received that email on a Monday. It was a vacuuming day and, as she finished her carpets and pressed herself against the handle as usual, she thought about Master G's email and her arousal spiked quickly. Too soon she had to pull the handle away in order to comply with Master G's orders, gasping and frustrated with the fleeting pleasure. *Get a hold of yourself*, she thought. Breathing deeply, she pressed her soft folds against the vibrations once again. The words in his email jumped into her mind. *You really are a horny little slut ... Somebody needs to take you in hand ... You may not cum.*

Oh God! Quickly, she pulled the handle away. She was nearly too late that time. And she'd barely held it there a minute! What the hell was happening to her?

Tuesday came and went with no emails or instant messages, as did Wednesday then Thursday. Shirley couldn't remember when it had been so long between contact. She was mad with frustration after continuing to use her vacuum for the much-needed pleasure of the vibrations, but with no release she was a throbbing mess. She went through the mundane chores of her life with unseeing automatic responses, constantly wet, Master G's words constantly running through her head.

On Friday, finally, when she sat down to her instant

message window at 10 a.m., lonely, desperate, aching, there he was.

Master G: I trust you've been following my instruction.

SexyShirley36: Yes, sir.

Master G: Very good. You've been using the vacuum?

SexyShirley36: Yes, sir.

Master G: And u haven't cum?

SexyShirley36: No, sir.

Master G: And how r u feeling?

SexyShirley36: Fine, sir.

A beat. A moment. And then:

Master G: I thought I was v clear in my email that I expect total honesty. U aren't fine. You're horny and desperate, aren't u?

SexyShirley36: Yes, sir.

Master G: Is ur pussy wet?

Oh, God. Shirley's cheeks burned bright with embarrassment. She couldn't respond. Didn't know how, couldn't type the words. After a moment with no response from her, Master G typed again.

Master G: I'm waiting.

SexyShirley36: Yes, sir. I'm very ...

It was all she could type, couldn't bring herself to even finish the sentence.

Master G: You're going to have to learn obedience, slut. You will not be coy and will tell me everything I ask when I ask it. I already know what a horny slut you are, there's no use pretending.

SexyShirley36: Yes, sir.

Master G: As punishment, tonight when ur husband fucks you, you still may not cum.

Oh. My. God. He couldn't be serious? Though she didn't have to ask to know just how serious Master G was.

In bed with Marcus that night was exquisite torture. At 9.30 p.m. as usual, he began with her nipples.

The usually slow and pleasurable build-up was replaced by an instantaneous spike in her arousal, sparks of sensation running straight from her hardened peaks to the throbbing bud of flesh between her legs. She tried to keep from gasping out, to make everything seem to progress normally, but her hips had a life of their own, pushing upwards and seeking pressure. Small whimpers escaped her lips.

As Marcus continued his fondling, Shirley continued to battle her body's responses. She was rigid, like a bow, and she practically held her breath to keep herself mute. She knew she couldn't even attempt to fake the little giggles and soft sighs that she usually made, could barely imagine, if she opened her mouth, the panting and wailing that would come out as her husband continued to tease her flesh with his fingers.

'Are you all right, my darling?' Marcus eventually said, taking his hand away from her breasts and laying it gently on her abdomen. 'You seem different tonight. Are you not in the mood?'

'I–I'm all right, sweetheart,' she managed to choke out.

'Are you sure?' he said as he absently rubbed his hand in small soft circles over her stomach and even this relatively innocent gesture made her insides flutter, caused the moisture that was seeping from between her legs to begin to flow. 'We don't have to do this if you don't want to. Or I could do this,' and he leant over her, taking a nipple between his lips.

Sensation shot through her core to her clitoris again as her husband's tongue flicked at her hyper-sensitive flesh. This time she couldn't hold the gasp back and, when he grazed the turgid nub with his teeth, giving her the gentle nibbling bites she normally moaned softly over, her hips bucked up and she cried out.

'Did I hurt you?' Marcus asked, raising his head.

'No, no,' Shirley said panting, 'I–I'm fine.'

'Do you want to stop?'

'No!' Shirley exclaimed, just a little too loudly. 'Sorry, I mean, it's not that at all. It's just ...' She paused, not knowing how to explain herself. 'I guess I'm just a little more ...eager, tonight.'

'What? You mean ...' Marcus started, reaching his hand down between his wife's thighs. He didn't even have to reach his fingers between the lips of her shaven sex, didn't get that far. Her outer labia themselves were slick with her arousal.

'My God, you're soaking wet!' Marcus said in amazement.

Shirley was nothing less than mortified. What Marcus must think of her! But how could she explain? He didn't know what her body had been through the past week, how it had been teased and primed and denied over and over for days and days. How could she admit now what Master G had done to her, *was* doing to her? And even more impossible to explain, what she couldn't understand herself, was how she was not only complicit but how she craved it.

But Marcus apparently needed no explanation, at least not then. He eagerly moved on top of his wife and began to enter her. Her wetness allowed him to slide in in one swift motion, meeting not a bit of resistance. Her pussy fairly sucked him inside.

'Oh, God, baby, you feel *so good*,' Marcus sighed, beginning to move slowly. He felt harder than usual and Shirley clung to his back, relishing his motions and his fullness inside her while trying desperately not to clench around him, not to push her aching clit against him, not to do any of the things that normally sent her over the edge. And also trying to clear her head of Master G's thrilling words.

After only a minute Marcus stopped.

'Geez, baby, I'm sorry, I'm not going to be able to last long tonight. You just feel so amazing,' he said.

Oh thank God, Shirley thought, her sex quivering around his hardness. She knew she couldn't have held out much longer. He began thrusting again but this time pushing her legs together and angling himself against her clit, the way he always made her come.

Oh no! She shoved her legs open again, wide as they would go, as one hard pulse tore through her, her orgasm looming dangerously, teetering. 'Babe, what are you doing?' Marcus gasped but continued to thrust inside her, past the point of no return himself. *You may not cum ...* Oh God. She tried desperately to clear her head and accept Marcus's thrusts while angling her body so as to limit his contact with her clit. But she was so close, just the feel of him moving inside her was too much. *You really are a horny little slut.* Oh fuck, she really was. *Do you need to cum that badly?* She was trying so hard to hold back but Master G's words pushed her closer, as much as her husband moving inside her. *Relax, relax your muscles*, she thought. I can do it. I can hold back.

Then Marcus grabbed her hands, held them, pinned, above her head. He shoved her legs together hard, immobilized between his and ground his pelvis firmly onto her, holding the base of his hard cock against her sensitive flesh and rotating his hips, rocking against her clit.

He leant down, his mouth against her ear and whispered, 'Mm, you like that don't you, slut?'

Holy shit.

Shirley's heart pounded in recognition and she let out a wail as her orgasm exploded out of her. Held firmly against the bed with no way to pull back from the delicious rocking pressure against her clitoris, her body finally betrayed her, reacting the only way it could to the intense sensations after being starved for so long. Wave after orgasmic wave poured over her as she felt Marcus pulse and shoot inside her.

After a moment Shirley, still dazed and confused, tried to talk.

'Marcus, did you say ...?'

'Shh, my little slut. In bed, from now on, you will call me "Master".'

Shirley could only stare in disbelief. Speechless, she swallowed hard, though her throat was dry.

'Now, I'll have to think of an appropriate punishment for this latest transgression. I'm considering something involving cucumbers ...'

Mean Girl
by Rachel Kramer Bussel

Leah surveyed the ad she'd just placed on Craigslist, smiling to herself as she reread the words she'd painstakingly crafted:

Mean Girl Seeks Bad Boy to Punish

Me: Mean girl, 33, long black hair, 5'9", curvy, black glasses.
You: 25-50, bad boy seeking punishment for your crimes. Be ready to confess, repent and take a beating. Creativity a plus.
I will expect an appropriate tribute.

She'd added the last bit after perusing other ads online, except those were from professional dominatrices, and Leah was only in it for the fun, for the rush, for the wetness the power to dominate a man gave her. Still, though, if she could get paid to do it, all the better, and she knew there were guys who'd take her more seriously if she asked for cash, kind of like the way she was willing to pay more for an outfit when it came from one of her favourite labels than some anonymous shop. Maybe doing this, with strangers she'd never see again, for money, arranged online, would help her get over her own ridiculous insecurities and turn her into the type of domme who wears her cruelty as proudly as her lipstick.

She thought about William, her recent ex, the last man she'd played with. They'd gone from a few relatively vanilla romps in bed before he'd confessed what he'd really wanted. She'd been kissing and licking his nipple, practically hidden amid his hairy chest, when he said, 'Harder.' She raised her head.

'What do you want me to do harder, William?'

'My nipple. Bite it. As hard as you want. Hurt me. Punish me, ma'am,' he said, his normally deep voice going high and almost girlish.

She did – or at least, she tried. She took the tiny hard nub between her lips and clamped down. She thought about how sensitive her own nipples were, how they could take seemingly endless licks of pain. She twisted the other nipple while she bit and after a few minutes ordered William onto her lap so she could give him a spanking. It had been fun but the next time she'd found that there was only so far she could go; he wanted her to hurt him, berate him, and scold him in ways she just wasn't prepared for, to punish him for imagined transgressions she just couldn't wrap her mind around.

She wanted to, very much so, because when she tied his wrists together and watched him squirm, then straddled his face and sank her pussy down onto his eager, happy mouth, she found that she loved it, far more than she ever had being on the other side. But she couldn't take his belt and lash his bottom, she couldn't bring herself to give him more than a light tap across his face, she couldn't bind his cock so tightly that it looked like it might explode, no matter how much she knew that's what he wanted.

They eventually broke up and she'd decided to see what happened with whoever she dated next. There were three more men, short-lived relationships, and all, once she really got to know them, secretly submissive. None were the types you'd ever suspect it of; on the outside, they were power hunks, one covered in tattoos, thin but muscular, one hefty and professional in his ever-present Wall Street-mandated suit, one a man who dominated every conversation he had – even ones he was simply overhearing. Yet beneath their male macho drag they all wanted the same thing and Leah, despite her burgeoning recognition of her innate female sexual power, couldn't seem to give it to them, not in the way they truly wanted. Hence, the personal ad. Maybe if the dating element, the interpersonal dance, were taken out of the equation, she'd be able to access her inner bitch goddess. She'd tried other methods of accessing her wildness and anger – boxing lessons at the gym, driving a friend's car in rush-hour Manhattan, a few highly recommended drugs, but nothing had really enabled her to let go of her good-girl golden rule roots.

It only took five minutes after she'd pressed submit before she started getting responses, and she soon found she liked the anonymity of the process, and the eagerness on the part of those writing to her to please. Maybe these men had a macho side when they were out on the street, but she didn't plan to see them outside of a room she was going to rent at the Maritime Hotel. They weren't going to know her name was Leah; to them, she was going to be Mistress Heather. She wasn't 28 or a grad student, but 33 and a personal trainer. She didn't have average mousy brown hair, but long black hair that fell to her ass. She didn't leave the house wearing only SPF 30 moisturizer and freckles, but rather a whole face full of make-up. She was, indeed 5'9" and curvy, but that would work to her advantage; the glasses were ones she'd bought to look more studious, but they'd help her look the part she needed now too. Mistress Heather was, perhaps, a girl Leah would want to fuck herself if she could, or at least hang out and get drunk with on a Saturday night.

Leah had told her best friend, Diane, about her experiment and Diane, always eager for a makeover project, had rustled up the perfect outfit for Mistress Heather and volunteered to paint her face. Leah booked a room for Friday and Saturday night, figuring she might as well get her money's worth – or rather, her clients'.

She surveyed the responses, needing to slip her fingers into her white cotton panties as she read tales of men who needed punishment for everything from embezzlement to cheating on their wives to eating all the ice cream in the freezer to simply being wretched human beings. She was sure some were making up their misdeeds, but it didn't matter; they felt like scum, and wanted her to treat them like it. She started shoving her fingers deep into her pussy, using her other hand to mark down on her notepad which men's missives had made her extra wet, which had gone beyond garden-variety neediness into territory that brought out the part of her that was a very mean girl indeed. With these strangers, she knew she didn't have to be her naturally cautious self, checking in incessantly and ruining the mood. They wanted her to beat them until they screamed, to lead them around on leashes, to expose them to strangers, to bind their wrists and other body parts? She was ready – or at least, Mistress Heather was.

Diane helped Leah get ready before she checked in at three that Friday, so she could stride into the lobby of the Chelsea hotel with confidence, gliding up the stairs and handing the doorman her credit card like she belonged there. The black dress wasn't skintight latex, sure to alert all to what she was really up to. It was a more refined look, with a black top, supple black skirt landing just at her knee, with expensive black Wolford tights and black and gold heels so high she had to practise.

Mistress Heather didn't really care if they thought she was a hooker or just some rich bitch – she had important business to conduct – but she wanted to feel at least a little herself in her outfit, not a caricature. It worked, and they led her to a suite where she closed the door behind her and surveyed her dossier on who was meeting her there. Tonight it was Al, followed by Rick, and tomorrow afternoon she had two more clients – or three, if you counted the couple who wanted her to punish both of them, while also giving the woman a little lesson in domination.

Leah admired the way the soft black leather skirt clung to her ass as she stripped off her top and bra, replacing it with a see-through off-white blouse she'd bought with tonight in mind. Any extra pounds she might have worried about in her regular life simply added to Mistress Heather's commanding persona. After all, you couldn't be a wisp of a girl and be a truly fierce domme, or if you could, Leah knew she wouldn't be able to pull that off. Her body gave her extra power, an added ability to bring grown men to their knees. Normally, she wanted, at least in her fantasies, to be petite and tiny, dwarfed by whichever man she was out with. Tonight, though, she wanted to be tall, large and in charge, and she shook out the silky long black wig she'd selected to go with her ensemble, too afraid to wear it before now. Adding it to her severely made-up face, with the dramatic red lipstick Diane had promised wouldn't wear off for 12 hours, along with the black eyeliner rimming each other, added to her sexpot look. Everything about her said, 'Don't fuck with me' – from the false eyelashes to the teetering heels that put her at the height she'd posted in the ad.

She put away all her belongings and sat on the bed, studying Al's responses. He'd been excessively polite; he was older, almost old enough to be her father, and wanted basically to be told what to do, which was good, because he would help ease her into the pain sluts. She got the impression that he was in a loveless marriage, or at least a lustless one. Looking in the mirror, Leah decided to pull some of her hair back with a barrette, to add a softer, feminine touch to the domme look she was working.

The bell rang. Al was a few minutes early, and looked

like he was ready for a night on the town. He was wearing a suit, his salt-and-pepper hair slicked back. He didn't look like her dad, but someone's, certainly.

'Hello,' she said, not yet having anything to properly rebuke him about. 'You are to refer to me as Mistress Heather, and you are not to touch me unless I tell you to. Do you understand?' she asked, pushing him to the ground as she spoke. She figured that, like jumping into freezing-cold water, she'd better plunge right in, lest she lose her nerve.

'Yes, ma'am. I mean, Mistress Heather.'

'I'll take your tribute now,' she said, holding out her hand, that act alone making her pussy pulse. As Al opened his wallet and removed $20 after $20 note, the crisp green bills made what they were doing all the more real. Leah had never been one for casual sex, and while this might not have technically fit the definition of either word, the money took the place of the surfeit of emotion she was used to.

'Very good,' she said, turning and deliberately bending over to place the money in her purse, giving Al a view of her leather-clad ass. She heard his breath quicken at the sight, and turned back around to find his hand on his cock. She pointedly looked down and he moved it to the side.

'Now, Al, I know from what you've told me that you are here to please me. What do you think it says about you that you've skipped ahead to touching your cock without asking me?'

His face blushed fiercely and his voice was quieter than it had been at first. 'I'm sorry, Mistress Heather. I didn't even realise I was doing it. I just got hard.' Though he had to be in at least his mid-50s, his voice was suddenly that of a boy's, high and nervous.

'I think you're old enough to know exactly what you're doing,' she snapped. 'Get on your knees, take out your cock for me, then put your hands behind your back.' She'd brought a cock ring in her arsenal, and now seemed like the perfect time to use it. Leah had to hold back a smile as she fastened it around him.

'Now let's see how good you are at taking orders.' She reached into her bag and brought out a timer, setting it for five minutes. 'You have five minutes to make me come with your tongue. Keep your hands behind your back. Forget about your cock, because it's not going anywhere near my pussy tonight. Ready?' she asked, though it wasn't really a question. Leah straddled the older man's face and felt him come into his own as she did. They wound up with him on the floor and her pressed down against him, only rising up occasionally to give him a few seconds of air, and though he made her come – twice – before the buzzer rang, he was so good at licking her that she stayed there for a while longer.

'You may have redeemed yourself,' she said, stroking his hair when she rose. 'Now crawl across the floor,' she demanded, and he did, even though she knew just how hard he was. When he crawled back toward her, the look on his face was priceless. She made him swallow her biggest dildo, loving the drool that pooled from his mouth as he endeavoured to take it all down his throat. He came close, and though she wanted to praise him, she knew that that's not what he truly wanted.

'That's it? Any 18-year-old girl could do better than that. I think you need to go to a sex shop immediately after you leave and buy a giant cock for yourself and practise sucking on it so that next time you can truly please me. Do you understand?'

His face was warm to the touch when she stroked him there, then pinched his pink cheek. He said yes, and she told him he should wear the cock ring out – she had more. 'Oh, thank you, ma'am, so, so much,' he said, before handing her another round of $20 bills and departing.

Leah hummed to herself once he was gone, and studied her notes. Rick was the one who'd wanted to be turned into a girl, and Leah had told him to bring what he needed to turn himself into Rickie, though she had a few added feminine touches. When he walked in, he looked like an average guy, skinny, shy, with a bit of dark stubble on his cheeks. She slapped one, liking the sting in her palm so much she did it again, feeling no qualms about the act whatsoever. 'Why didn't you shave before you got here? You're just wasting my time and yours,' she barked as she called room service for a razor. 'Before they get here, quick, pucker your lips,' she said, the idea coming to her instantly. Rick instantly did as she'd ordered, and she painted his lips a deep, dark red. 'Now smile,' she said, and he did, though he was clearly unused to dressing up in front of anyone else, let alone someone like her. There was a knock at the door.

'Answer it, and tell the man that the razor is for you,' she said, smiling to herself as Rick's face changed to a colour that would guarantee she wouldn't need blush on him.

Rick opened the door and his face paled, but the bellhop didn't blink. 'Thank you,' Rick said. 'It's for me – for the stubble. I'm a crossdresser,' he blurted, and the man smiled and simply waited for a tip. Rick fumbled in his pocket and produced a five, and the bellhop looked at Leah over his shoulder and winked.

When it was back to just the two of them, Rick looked like he was on the verge of tears. 'Wow,' he said. 'That was amazing.'

'That was nothing,' she corrected, before producing the pink layered prom-like dress Diane had found for her at a thrift shop. Rick's eyes widened, and when he looked like he was going to protest, she put her hand over his mouth. 'I'm in charge now,' she said. 'You're not only going to wear this – after you shave – but you're going to go downstairs and bring me back a drink. A nice, girlie cosmopolitan – pink to match your dress.'

She looked down and saw his dick was rock hard. Impulsively, she kissed Rickie, even though that wasn't really part of the game, it just felt right. That was something she was coming to understand about being a true domme –

there were no rules. She could do whatever she wanted, she could even get on all fours and get fucked hard, and still do it as Mistress Heather, if she believed hard enough. Her power was there for her to claim, and as Rickie dressed for her, dolling herself up into the girl she wanted to be, Leah smiled and knew she was making progress.

She sent Rickie down to the bar and then went to the bathroom and just stared at herself, admiring the way her breasts looked through the blouse, feeling the sensual curve of her ass, encased in the leather. She shut her eyes and pictured the entire bar bowing down to her, needing just a smile to have men rushing from all corners to do her bidding. The knock on the door startled her at first, but she immediately composed herself.

Through the hole in the door, Rickie looked so obedient and eager that she melted a little, not slipping up and revealing Leah, but seeing the tenderness inside Mistress Heather. She opened the door and Rickie's eyes sought hers out. 'How did it go?' she asked. 'Did they know?'

'I don't know, Mistress, but I don't think so.' She reached for the glass and took a long sip, surveying her client. 'Get on the floor and rub my feet,' she said as she sank onto the bed and sipped her cocktail. 'Sing to me.' Singing seemed like an appropriately feminine activity, and soon she was getting both a foot massage and a lullaby. She was already mentally giving Rickie a makeover, taking her shopping, surreptitiously groping her cock. This was supposed to be a strictly financial transaction, which was fine for Mistress Heather, but less so for Leah. She'd never been with a woman before but suddenly so many new possibilities blossomed before her eyes. When she'd drained her glass, she pushed Rickie's foot away. 'Show me your panties,' she said, and Rickie obeyed, lifting up the many ruffled layers to reveal pink lacy panties and a decidedly unladylike erection. Their hour was almost up but she knew what she wanted.

'Come closer,' Leah said, softly, and began massaging Rickie's cock. It wasn't in the game plan for the evening, but that didn't matter. She wanted to feel him – her – both beings at once. 'Don't tell anyone I did this,' she said in a harsh whisper as she reached into Rick's panties and stroked his cock. She didn't need to see it, just to hold it, to embrace both sides of her soul too, the timid, tender part of Leah and the roughness of Mistress Heather.

'Of course not, Mistress,' Rick said in a deep voice, and then the only sound in the room was a few minutes of his heavy breathing before she expertly coaxed the come out of him. She wiped her hand on his leg, and then offered him her palm to lick it up. He did so daintily, elegantly, which she respected. She let him keep the dress if he promised to wear it home – and call her again.

The next morning Leah got up and hit the gym hard, running and lifting weights, pumping herself up for the day to come, her mind astir with fantasies. Leah had found the day before that the more the men obeyed her, the more she relaxed into being Mistress Heather, no longer sucking her stomach in and rehearsing what she was going to say. Even better, she actually liked it, finding that she took her cues from them to a degree, but that there was something inside her that got off on just how naughty all this was. She was taking their money to order them around, slap them, get foot massages; how crazy was that? It also turned her on, and she found herself remembering moments, snapshots from the past where she'd ridden a man and held his arms down, where she'd ordered him not to come until she was ready. Maybe her exes had just gone too fast for her, asked too much from her.

She focused on Steve, her late-afternoon client, a self-proclaimed "pain slut". He wanted her to go to town on him, to kick him and slap him and hurt him. He had a safeword all picked out – "rainbow" – but it sounded like there was little chance he'd use it. She was the one who had to work up the courage to give him what he wanted. He was paying her twice her fee, having offered her a thousand-dollar tribute for two hours, which she couldn't refuse. But still, she'd wanted to be prepared. She'd bought special gloves that seemed soft and sensual but had hidden spikes. She'd gotten a Wartenberg wheel and candles to drip hot wax on him. The biggest preparation, though, was in her mind.

When he arrived, Leah was back in Mistress Heather mode, the latex once again clinging to her, a new pair of even taller, more severe black heels on her feet. He was a little taller than her, but the deep breath she took and her new perspective made it seem the opposite. He handed her an envelope and then, without a word, she slammed the door and slapped his face. He let out a strangled cry and she did it again, already reaching for his cock. They didn't need any foreplay, and there wasn't time. Her next clients were coming immediately after he was done.

She turned Steve around and slammed his face against the door. 'Put your hands over your head.' He did, and she went to fetch the Swiss army knife she always kept in her purse. 'Shut your eyes,' she commanded, and she ran the knife's edge along his skin. He'd indicated in his email that he liked to make noise, that his inclinations even scared him a little, and she'd had to wrap her mind around that. Did she want him to look scared, or look like he liked it? For Steve, they were one and the same, so she trained herself to enjoy the way he seemed to inch away from her. She tore his blue shirt with the knife, getting excited at the noise. She ripped the rest with her bare hands, then used her newly elongated red nails, fresh from the salon, to rake them down his back. 'I'm glad you mark so well,' she said, then slapped his back hard with her hand.

She struck his back hard, sending him closer to the door's surface, only stopping when her hand tingled and she heard him whimpering; the noise had been indiscernible while she was hitting him. Leah had all sorts of implements at her disposal, but her hand was her favourite. With it she could dig her nails into his back, place her palm over his mouth, pinch his nipple or slap his cock. She could pinch his cheek, lightly at first, as she did once she turned him around, then harder and harder, as if taunting him to try to protest. It was the best tool she had at her disposal, one that was, when it came right down to it – no matter how much was in the envelope sitting on the dresser – priceless.

She made him turn around and look at her, really look at her, even though he tried to shut his eyes. 'Open your eyes, show me how much I've made you cry.' The words would've been foreign to the old Leah, but this one, the one who'd come this far, who'd turned herself into the kind of woman who did kink on command, for money, liked seeing a man much larger than her cower in, not fear, exactly, but something more primal, more powerful. And he wasn't cowering, she realised when he finally met her gaze. He was thanking her. She tugged on his lower lip and brought her knee between his legs, pressing upward, keeping her eyes trained on him. When she'd had her fill, she let go, ordering him to strip.

She smiled to herself when she saw how big his cock was. She wasn't a size queen, exactly, but she liked them big; it gave her more to work with, even if she wasn't planning to put his dick anywhere inside her. It was also a reverse kind of pride, because a man with a cock so well-formed, so perfect, would usually think of himself as the type to get any girl he wanted. But Steve didn't want just any girl, didn't want to be the macho, manly stud. He wanted the reverse; he wanted what she was doing now, which was spitting on his dick, and then slapping it. She felt as well as heard him wince. 'Why are you here, Steve?' she barked.

She pushed him onto the bed, his face slammed against the bedspread, then picked up the riding crop and slapped it hard against his cheeks, one and then the other. 'Ow,' he cried, and she hit him even harder.

'It's supposed to hurt. Now answer my damn question.'

He sputtered, but finally replied. 'I'm here because I need you to hurt me. I like to be hurt. I want it, I crave it, it makes me feel like this is where I belong.' While he rambled on, she kept going, down his thighs, tapping his calves, turning him over to whack his nipples. She only had to flick the tip of the crop lightly against his balls to make him practically come. She was getting close herself, but this was more important – and not just to Steve.

'Put this on,' she spat, shoving a fur-trimmed blindfold at him. He scrambled to get it on while she pulled out her lighter and found herself breathing heavily as she took out the maroon candle, lighting it and then watching the beautiful flame flicker. 'Are you ready, Steve?' she asked. There was only one right answer to that question.

'Yes, Mistress Heather,' he said, and she tilted the candle just enough so a line of wax formed on his chest. The whimpering started up again, and the tears, and she brought the candle closer, intent on using it all up.

'Do you like that, Steve? Do you like the pain?' She knew he did – they both knew – but she wanted to hear him say it.

'Yes, I like the pain you give me, Mistress.' The rest of the session seemed to fly by, after she covered as much of him in wax as she could. He washed it off so she could take his freshly washed back and apply the special glove, knowing that she pressed just hard enough to break the skin, and that he'd have to walk out of there without a shirt. When her alarm went off, she squeezed his cock as hard as she could while slamming four fingers into his mouth, loving every hit of power she took from his body. When she told him their time was up, he looked like he was in a daze. 'Thank you, Mistress Heather,' he said quietly, then got dressed, abandoning the shirt, not even asking about it.

He left and Leah gave herself a few minutes to cool

down. She looked out the window and saw the world of Chelsea below, the city bustling, but she was perfectly fine right there in that room. She hadn't realised just how intense the sessions would be, way more so than her previous attempts at kink. Because she was no longer timid, afraid of her power, she had known exactly what to do.

Dylan and Lisa arrived and looked like your average fresh-scrubbed college students, though they were actually both in their late 20s. She seemed to have come straight from a tennis court in a pleated skirt and simple white top, her hair in a ponytail. 'So you both like to bottom, do you?' she asked, surveying their reactions. Lisa practically curtsied, while Dylan said, simply, 'Yes.'

'Yes what?' she asked. 'Don't you mean, "Yes, Mistress"?'

She walked right up next to him, grateful for the added height so she could stare down at him. 'Yes, Mistress,' he said, and she could feel his erection through his jeans.

'You are going to learn some manners today. But first you're going to go sit in that chair while I have some fun with your girl here.' She hadn't planned to separate them, but suddenly she wanted Lisa across her lap, wanting to see how big – and sensitive – her breasts were, how badly she wanted it. Dylan hadn't moved, and looked like he wanted to say something. 'Do you have a problem with that? Do you not like the way I'm running this session? The first rule of submission, Dylan, is that you have to accept that you are not in charge, and don't deserve to be. If you can't handle that, then you can leave now and I can focus solely on your pretty, slutty lady here.' She'd thrown in "slutty" to taunt him, to see if he tried to rise to her defence. He didn't. He slinked back to the corner and she pulled Lisa close.

The girl had blonde ringlets that added to her innocent appearance, but when Leah, who'd removed her nail extensions between sessions, reached under her skirt, she found that Leah was going commando. 'Such a wet pussy for such an innocent-looking girl,' she said, holding her by the throat while she shoved two fingers into her pussy. 'Dylan, have you been fucking her enough?' It was a clearly rhetorical question; either way, Mistress Heather was going to claim Leah tonight.

Leah pulled Lisa back to the bed and splayed her over her lap, lifting up the skirt. The girl's bottom was round and ripe and perfect, and again, she used her hand to spank it. The skin was deliciously smooth, a contrast to the men she'd been seeing, and her pulse pounded harder as her newfound lesbian longings, activated by Rickie the day before, came to the fore. 'Sometimes, to be a good slave, you have to be patient,' she said, looking right at Dylan as she smacked Lisa's ass over and over. 'Do you understand?'

Dylan nodded as she pulled Lisa's hair, making her whimper. Lisa squirmed but didn't try to stop her. She knew their safewords too, had insisted on them via email, but Lisa, for all her outward struggle, clearly loved being spanked, because when Leah smacked her sleek pussy, the girl went wild. 'So, Lisa, you want to know how to be a domme? Or maybe you just want a domme for yourself?'

'Yes,' was the answer she got, and she tossed Lisa onto the ground. 'Take off all your clothes and sit on your knees with your hands behind your back.' It was a look that made anyone, male or female, more attractive. Leah went into the closet and hurriedly unzipped the dress, her sweaty skin now free, and slipped into the harness she'd purchased, along with a fat purple dildo, the only one in the store that had truly spoken to her.

She walked out and told Dylan to strip and join Lisa. Then, with both of them kneeling before her, Mistress Heather fed them her cock – or fucked their faces; both phrases were totally accurate. Lisa was better at deepthroating, able to rock on her heels and put her whole body into the movement, while Dylan seemed to struggle, at least, until she grabbed his head and forced her way there.

She could see his dick was hard and upright, so she kept going, batting the dick against their cheeks, teasing them with the head, loving every second of it. She'd never thought she'd be the strap-on type – it had seemed too butch, too much – but it was simply the coup de grâce to this whole exercise in claiming her natural power.

'Whose mouth is this?' she asked, slapping each of them simultaneously, Dylan with her left hand, Lisa with her right.

'Yours, Mistress Heather,' they said in unison, and she smiled. 'Dylan, lie down on your back,' she said, and when he did, she placed Lisa over his face, shoving her down. While Lisa rode her man, Leah toyed with her nipples, pinching and twisting and tugging on them, marvelling at just how fun a woman's body was, how much she had to work with. 'Let him know you own him,' she said, and they shared a searing look, one of knowledge passing between two women who know they're infinitely smarter than the man in the room.

She rose and retired to the bed to stroke her cock, feeling the pressure not only in her clit but deep inside, in her core, as she watched Lisa turn from a hungry girl with her mouth open to one who knew that demanding pleasure and service was her right. While Lisa straddled Dylan's cock, Leah fucked herself, no longer amazed that she could get paid for this, but that she hadn't thought of it sooner.

Later, when she was alone, she went online, and set up a profile for herself on a kinky dating site. Maybe she could even try this for real. Her screen name? Mean Girl NYC.